Author

LANI YOUNG

Scarlet
Redemption

Part Three of the **Scarlet Series**

Scarlet Redemption

LANI YOUNG

AUTHOR'S NOTE

IN MEMORY OF PEKA
WHO SHOWED ME HOW GOD LOVES.

Prologue

When we were small, Aunty Filomena would tell us fagogo. If Mother was in the room, the fagogo were all from the Bible. A mishmash of Jesus feeding the multitude with loaves and fishes, Daniel in the lion's den and the ten wise virgins. Mother would nod and smile with sanctimonious approval, adding in her lua sene worth every so often. She especially liked Bible stories with women in them and would give Aunty Filomena reminders when she stalled. Or she would butt in and take over altogether. Unlike Aunty, Mother's fagogo always had a moral added to them, that she elaborated on at length. Just in case we missed them.

"Bathsheba – remember girls, that's what happens when a woman doesn't live a modest life. King David was such a righteous man that even God himself said David was a man after his own heart. But Bathsheba tempted him beyond what a man can handle. Flaunting her nakedness like that. You must never forget the power that your body can have on a righteous man. It's your responsibility to be the purifying influence that a man needs."

"Delilah." A grimace. "Look what happened to poor Samson, what Delilah did to him with her manipulative evil ways." And off she would go, reciting the lurid tale of

Samson's demise.

I myself always thought that Samson was a wimpy loser so easily tricked. All muscle and no brains. Delilah was clever and impressed me with her smarts. *Now there's a girl that will go far in life!* I kept that to myself of course. It wouldn't do for the daughter of a faifeau to admit that she fan-girled the skanky Delilah after all.

I would have preferred to hear about Jael the warrior who delivered the people of Israel by driving a stake through Sisera's forehead. Or Deborah the kickass Prophetess. But they were the kind of Biblical women that Mother preferred to pretend didn't exist.

We sisters knew better than to make any edits or contributions when Mother was doing the fagogo. Instead we would listen and nod with pious silence as we worked on our crocheting, making doily cloths for the church altar. Mother insisted that we learn all the Christian missionary womanly arts – cooking, sewing, embroidery as well as crochet. She let Aunty teach us how to weave mats but only because ie toga were making a resurgence and she wanted us to be able to join the annual parading of fine mats with the other women of the village. It would be shameful for her if we didn't participate. So our evenings were spent on industrious crafts, made bearable by storytelling.

But as soon as Mother was out of hearing, we would pester Aunty for the *real* fagogo. The stories she kept hidden in her heathen heart. Stories of blood clots and stalker eels that terrorized girls called Sina. Dangerously beautiful aitu like Telesa who lured unsuspecting fair-haired men to vague illicit activities in the bush. The giant Vaea who wept for his love Apaula and turned into a mountain. The rascally Ti'iti'i who used sly ingenuity to bring us fire from the earthquake god. We could listen to her fagogo for hours.

My favorite was of Nafanua. But I didn't like to share it with the others. No. I would wait until they had drifted to sleep and then I would snuggle a little closer to Aunty and ask her for the story of the war goddess. Like any good fagogo, there were many variations of the Nafanua story, but I had my preferred version – the one Aunty Filomena had woven just for me, based on all my suggestions and questions. This is why I love fagogo. Because the best tellers weave the tale to suit the listener. And Aunty Filomena was one of the best. She would sit a little taller, clear her throat and assume the solemn tone that she reserved for the greatest of all the warriors in our history.

Nafanua didn't have a mother. Not really anyway. That could be what first endeared her story to me. She was a blood clot, found in the ocean by Saveasiuleo, the god of Pulotu – what the palagi would call, the 'underworld'.

Saveasiuleo raised Nafanua as his own. He taught her how to fight, how to lead, navigate by the stars, recognize the best moon for planting, how to make fire, hunt, carve, make canoes, houses and shark traps, how to strategize and know your enemy better than yourself. By the time she was ten years old, Nafanua had mastered every weapon from the shark tooth war club to the finely woven garrote cord. She knew every plant for healing, and every leaf and root for poison. She knew the faalupega for every village and could recite the gafa and ancestral origin for every family in Samoa. She was skilled in oratory and could entrance any audience with her storytelling. In short, Saveasiuleo taught Nafanua everything she needed to know so she could be the greatest chief and warrior the earth had ever seen.

In our retelling of the fagogo, Saveasiuleo wasn't the terrifying demon of the usual legends. Sure he was strong and fierce and could assume the form of a giant eel. But he was also kind and loving, funny and fond of jokes, protective of his daughter and incredibly proud of her. (Yes, I'm well aware that a therapist would point out that Saveasiuleo was everything that my own father was not. Let's not go there right now.)

Nafanua was everything that Mother didn't want us to be. The kind of Samoan woman that the missionaries had tried their best to eradicate. In my mind's eye Nafanua looked a lot like Serena Williams and the warrior guards in the Black Panther movie. And with a generous measure of the captain of the New Zealand women's rugby team, the Black Ferns. But she had my face. (Of course.) And unlike me, she wasn't afraid. Of the dark. Of the auntie's whispers in jeering corners. Of centipedes. Or of the bite of the salu when Mother got angry. Nafanua wasn't even afraid of God. (Who we knew looked like Father with a Moses beard.) Because she was a god herself and didn't need to bow to anyone. God or man. Or Jesus.

But she was still a girl of flesh and bone amongst spirits in Pulotu and Nafanua had always longed to visit the world of mortals. The question was, how was she to get there? How do you go from the spirit world to the land of the living? She asked her father often but he would tell her to be patient. "You are not ready my child. Wait. Learn. Train. Prepare. One day."

Finally, the day came when she was able to make that journey. There was a war happening on Savaii and the people cried out for deliverance. Saveasiuleo decided it was time for Nafanua to ascend and take her place as the leader he had prepared her to be. Before she left he gave her gifts. War clubs, intricately carved and infused with the love, hopes and fears of a father for his beloved child. And he instructed her how to make the means of her passage, using the sacred wood of the Toa tree.

Nafanua followed his instructions. She cut down a toa tree and over many days and nights, she forged the Ulimasao, stripping the wood of its bark, sanding and polishing it to perfection. Fashioned in the shape of a paddle, she would use it to traverse the endless, treacherous waters that separate Pulotu from the land of the living. And once she got there, she would use it's merciless precision and power to slay her foes. Her father taught her the words to chant over the Ulimasao as she carved it and together their song would resonate through the fire-lit darkness. But there was only so much Saveasiuleo could do in the making of the Ulimasao because it needed to be Nafanua's weapon. Her journey. Her strength and courage that would take her from Pulotu to the above world. It would be she alone to wield it. And she alone would be responsible for the destruction it wrought.

"Remember my child," said Saveasiuleo as he farewelled Nafanua. "A true warrior knows there is a time to fight, to kill. And a time for mercy. A time to walk away. The key is knowing the difference."

I think about that Ulimasao often. How a paddle can serve as a weapon. How it can take one from a place of darkness, a place of spirit where one is unburdened by the feelings and cares of a physical body, to a place of light, both golden and freeing.

I often ask myself, how do we fashion our own Ulimasao? A paddle that can take us from our places of darkness and deadness – to a place of light and life? I wonder, where is my Toa tree? Can a person be that for us? Or is it a journey that one must take alone? And why would you want to?

There is safety in the dark. A kind of comfort in the absence of light and knowing and seeing. Remembering hurts.

Turning your face to the sun is painful.

Why would you want to?

CHAPTER *One*

unty Filomena knows what's wrong with me even before I do. It's the vomit that gives me away. I'm throwing up in the bathroom for the third time this week. Quietly so Mother doesn't hear me. But Aunty Filomena does. She's waiting for me in the hall when I open the door. A look of gentle sadness in her eyes.

"Scar, you ma'i." It's not a question.

Sick. Yes, I'm sick. I nod my head and it's a signal for the tears to come. Aunty enfolds me in her arms and soothes me as I sob on her shoulder.

"Aua te popole," she says, "Everything will be alright."

She asks me awkward questions. About my bleeding. When was the last time? I don't know.

She tells Mother for me. While I sit in the corner, waiting. I've heard the horror stories. The whispered faikala'ring of aunties and cousins, about what happens to bad girls who do bad things and get pregnant. Cousin Tisa got a big stomach when she was still in school. Thus ruining her chances for the Miss Samoa pageant that everybody always said she would be a sure win for. Her boyfriend was the Head Boy of Samoa College and very handsome. She tried to hide it for as long as possible. Until they couldn't dismiss it as her eating too many keke pua'a. Tisa was expelled. Her aunties shaved all her hair off. Her father beat her so bad the whole village could hear her screams for help. Father has never beaten any of us. I wonder if this will be when he uses more than words to punish one of his daughters?

Mother gasps loudly. Then she comes at me, a wild light in her eyes. I shrink back. Aunty Filomena steps in between us, holding mother away as her arms flail at me.

"No," she tells Mother. "She's just a child. Leave her."

Mother wilts in Aunty Filomena's arms. Cries. I am sad for her. Part of me feels guilty that I have brought this shame on her.

The rest of me feels nothing. Thinks nothing. Says nothing.

I am not here. I am far away. I am Nafanua in Pulotu. I'm not leaving. No Toa tree for me. I am the darkness and the darkness is me.

Mother doesn't ask me who made me ma'i. But I tell her anyway. She flinches and slaps my face before Aunty can stop her.

"Never say that again. You hear me? Filthy liar. I told

you before not to spread lies about your Uncle."

I'm scared of what Father will do to me when she tells him but she surprises me. Mother forbids Aunty to speak of my pregnancy to anyone. Especially not to Father. She takes me to the house with a three-legged dog outside. Where the grim faced woman makes me hurt. Makes me scream, muffled sounds against the ripped piece of lavalava that they have tied across my mouth to keep me quiet. Makes me bleed. Gushing rushes of blood. I think I am dying. In the blurred haze of pain that seems to last an eternity, I want to die. Mother anchors me to this earth. Pinches me with vicious ferocity as she tells me to BE QUIET.

"This is what you get for being a bad girl," she mutters against my ear. "A dirty girl who sins against God."

Then to the abortionist she says piously, "So many prayers for this girl, so much teaching her and still she goes astray, but we will never give up on this lost sheep."

There's a look of disgust on the severe woman's face. She turns to me with the first hint of compassion in her dark eyes. "It's nearly finished," she says. "Be strong."

Finally it is finished. The evening shadows are coming and Mother is impatient to go home. Father will be expecting her to serve his dinner.

The woman washes her hands in the paipa and explains to mother what medicine I need, what we should do to prevent infection – but Mother doesn't listen. She pays the woman with a fistful of money then hustles me out to the car.

The Bible says God sees everything. You can't hide anything. No act is unseen. No sin goes unpunished. It was foolish of mother to think otherwise. To presume that Father would not find out. Father was God's mouthpiece after all. He spoke for God, he acted for God. His wrath was inevitable. God's justice is over all.

The police come to our house. I am playing aki with my sisters in the back fale. Cross-legged on the dusty ground, arranged in a circle as we each take turns to expertly wield the aki stones we have gathered over several years. It's not easy to find five stones that can fit in the palm of your hand, and still be used for a game of aki. They can't be river smooth or flat because then you can't pick them up easily. They need to have ridges and texture. But not too much because then they hurt when you catch them. They need some weight to them too. If they're too lightweight than you will throw them too high. And of course the five stones must complement each other, ridged contours fitting into each other so they're a neat bundle in your closed fist.

Tamarina nudges my arm – which makes me falter and miss my aki stone. "Look what you did!" I snap at her, ready to fight for my right to have another turn.

She points and mouths, *Leoleo.*

Me and Naomi turn to look as three police get out of their truck and go inside. Two men and a woman in blue uniforms.

They meet with father in his study for a long time and when they leave, father calls for mother to join him. And then me. I need to go toilet, but it doesn't seem like the right moment to say so.

"Scarlet," he points to a spot beside the bookshelf. "Stand over there."

Mother is in a chair in the centre of the room. Crying silently.

Father sits behind his desk, formal and severe.

"What did you do?" he asks mother, with his calm, measured voice. "The police. Tell me their story is lies. Tell me."

More silent tears.

I am often afraid of Father, but today, I am afraid for mother. There's a purple vein bulging in father's right temple. The one that always threatens to pop when he's giving a particularly vehement sermon. His fingers are tightly clenched on his pen. The one stamped with *Oxford University, Faculty of Theology and Religion*. It's his favorite pen and I'm worried he's going to snap it. Will Oxford send him another one?

I wish mother would answer. Say something.

Father is impatient. He stands and thunders in his STRIKE YOU DOWN voice, "Speak woman. It's lies, isn't it? Tell me you didn't do this." He turns to me, "Did your mother take you to that place of murder? Of evil?"

My every thought stutters. *What place? Where? What's he talking about?* I throw mother a panicked look. Does she understand? Help.

"Answer me Scarlet!"

"I don't know," I say.

Mother whispers into the tightly bound quiet. "It's true. I took her there. To see that nurse."

Then I know what Father's talking about. *God sees everything.*

Father recoils. "Murderer," he says. He walks around the desk so that he's standing in front of mother. He hits her. A swift backhand to the face. *No sin goes unpunished.*

The sound is a splintered rupture of everything I know about our world, about who my parents are. I have never seen Father hit our mother before. He's never hit us children either. Mother is the giver of the biting hot salu sting. The one who pinches us viciously in church if we are restless. And fuki's our hair on the rare occasions that we dare answer her back.

There is a scream clawing inside me that wants to get out. Mother sways in her seat and her cheek is flushed red. Father's ring has cut her lip and there's blood. She wipes it away with a quick movement of her hand.

Father turns to me. Advances. "And you. My own flesh and blood. Only fourteen. Harlot. How could you do this thing?" With each word and each step closer, his voice gets louder. A righteous lion that rages and roars against wickedness. *God's wrath is inevitable.*

I'm afraid. He's going to hit me. Beat me. Hurt me. I squeeze my eyes shut, fists clenched tight by my sides. There's a hot stream running down my legs. Shame. I am a fourteen year old who pees her pants. *Moepi.*

I'm waiting, steeling myself for the blow that doesn't come.

"No!" Mother is up off her seat and by my side. Her fingers dig into my shoulders as she pushes me half-behind her. "Don't. Please."

She motions to the open windows. The breeze that carries every word, every sound to every curious cousin making the saka in the cookhouse, and every faikala neighbour who looks to the faifeau's house for Jesus' example. A hissed reminder, "What will people say?"

Father shakes his head as the fury seeps out of him.

I am something he's never seen before. Something he

can't bear to be in the same room with. He goes back to sit behind the desk. There's no more emotion as he explains why the police came to see him.

It's about the house that mother took me to. With the three-legged dog outside. The house where I learned there's something that hurts more than what Uncle Solomona shoved inside me all those many times.

The police found the house with the three-legged dog. They arrested the musu face woman with the gentle hands.

"There was a notebook," says Father. "She kept a record of all her clients. That's how they knew to come here."

The police are not after us though. It's been decided not to prosecute the women who visited the house, as long as they help with the case. Father spits that out.

Is he sorry we haven't been marched out in handcuffs?

They are gathering evidence. Witnesses who can testify at the abortionist's trial.

I taste vomit at the back of my throat. A trial? Where everyone will look at me and know?

Mother says, panicked. "No. We can't do that. What will people say?"

Father says we don't have a choice. Be a part of the prosecution's case, or else we could end up going to prison ourselves. "You took a life," he reminds us. "You killed an innocent unborn child."

He gazes out the window for a long while. *Maybe God's out there?* A deep breath. "Let us pray."

I auto sit and bow my head when what I really want to do is go change my pants. The pee smell stains the air yellow.

Father prays a long prayer. Exhorts God for His wisdom, justice and patience as he faces these trials and tribulations that his family have brought upon him.

"Can the blood of the Lamb wash us clean, oh Lord? How can it cleanse an evil such as this?" he intones.

Mother says a loud AMENE when he's done.

Father makes an announcement. "I must resign from my position. God has spoken it."

Mother makes a whimpering cry, *Oi Aue!* and begins sobbing loudly. She is distraught at this decision. But she doesn't question it. God has spoken. (We should probably be thankful God's still deigning to speak to us at all by this point.)

"I don't wish to speak of this again," says Father. He tells mother to 'sort this matter out' with her sister who's the Attorney General. And cautions, "You will need to seek your own path back to the Lord. I cannot help you."

More wailing from mother. Father is putting up a wall between her and God's grace. A wall that all the sewing of sheets for Mapuifagalele resthome, and the making of glorious floral arrangements for the church, cannot hope to scale.

He doesn't address me at all. I'm in outer darkness. Not even within sight of a wall to pray at.

"Leave me now. I must work on my resignation sermon."

Mother doesn't tell him what happened to me after the abortion. The infection that raged like fire. The ice cold cloths Aunty Filomena bathed me with as she wept, as she pleaded with mother to take me to the hospital. The sickness that devoured my insides, a shark eating all the babies that would never be, the emergency operation that left me empty but alive. I want Father to know. If he knows, maybe there will be kindness in his eyes, pity. Something, anything.

Father doesn't ask who was the father of my ma'i. I want him to ask. I'm determined to speak the words, if he asks. If he knows, than maybe he can forgive me? If he knows, maybe he can mediate with God for me?

Mother tugs at my arm and I stumble out of Father's office.

I look back at him, already hard at work writing and weighing words, and for the first time I question.

Maybe God doesn't see everything?

That evening, Father has his first stroke.

Mother finds him. When she goes to take his dinner on a tray. A scream that brings the household running. All of us crowding into the office, peering around each other. Father lies on the ground, eyes wide open, a slight twitch shuddering through him. Globs of spit on his chin. Naomi wails loudly and pulls at my hand, under the mistaken idea that her Big Sister can fix this. Tamarina just stares. Eyes wide and solemn as always, a slight frown on her face.

Mother catches sight of us at the door. "You!" She comes at me, pushing past the assorted boy cousins who have brought the umukuka smoke smell with them. They part like the Red Sea before her. "See what you did to your father?" she screeches.

Her hand draws back and then she hits me across the face. It's the blow Father didn't strike. Before the shock of the pain even registers, she hits me again. It hurts. There's a rushing roaring sound in my ears and the room looks fuzzy. Then Mother is shaking me. Like when our dog Rocky caught the neighbor's cat in his mouth. Shaking it until it was a broken bloody mess.

"Pa'umuku! Your filthy ways have done this to your father," she screams. "All your fault. You should never have been born. Maimau lo'u alofa. My love has been wasted on you."

The words come at me from a faraway place. I try to drop to my knees, to hide, to get away from the blows, away from everyone, but mother's grip doesn't let me.

Then it stops. The cousins are pulling Mother away and Aunty Filomena is there, shushing the tempest and ushering me out of the room.

Talofa e," she says. "Everything will be alright. Be a good girl Scar, be strong. Be a good girl."

I don't cry. I hold tight to the knowledge that Aunty Filomena loves me. That she will always love me. Even though it's too late for me to be a good girl.

Be a good girl. Be strong.

It's what Aunty tells me before I meet with the Judge. My nightmares of standing in a crowded courtroom being forced to recite my sins while people throw stones at me didn't eventuate. Instead the Judge meets with me in her office, because I'm underage. Mother comes too. I'm ready with the plastic lie for when the Judge asks me where my ma'i came from, but she never asks that. She only wants to know about the musu face woman with the bony hands. What did she do. What did she say. That's all.

Be a good girl. Be strong.

It's what Aunty tells me when the story comes in the newspaper and sets everyone's tongues on fire. My name isn't in there so I should be happy. But this is Samoa. We only keep some things secret, like when uncles rape their nieces. That's a secret nobody wants to hear. But a cheeky girl who gets pregnant and then kills her baby? Now that's a secret worth sharing.

I go to school and there are whispers and dirty looks. My friend Lisa is angry at me.

"Why didn't you tell me?" she demands.

"Tell you what?"

"That you had a boyfriend?"

I go to the toilet and someone has scrawled on the wall with magic marker.

Scarlet pa'umuku. Whore.

The Principal calls for a meeting with Mother but she is busy with Father at the hospital, so Aunty Filomena comes to school in a taxi. I wait outside the office and try not to scuff my seevae kosokoso, a nervous habit that always gets me a vicious pinch from Mother when we're in church.

When Aunty comes out of the meeting, her face is angry, her mouth a thin line. She grabs my hand. "Come

Scar, we go. Bring your bag."

Aunty is never angry at us. But could it be she is angry at me today? We get in the taxi and she snaps at the driver. When he drives carelessly through a jerky pothole, Aunty swears at him which tells me she's very angry because Aunty never curses anyone in front of us.

Auntie's constancy was the rock that we three girls walked on. No matter what happened, no matter what we did or said, we knew Auntie would always love us, fight for us and try to soothe our hurts with koko alaiasa and pani popo.

But here now, with the school growing smaller in the distance, it seems I may finally have reached the end of Auntie's love.

I'm crying.

I feel Auntie's anger and I cry. There can be no hope for my redemption if Aunty has given up on me.

We get to the house and Aunty only pays the driver half the fare. They argue. It's a battle I know he will lose. Aunty ignores his words and pulls me out of the car.

"Come Scar. We go."

The taxi driver swears at us as he drives off. "Aikae!"

Aunty picks up a handful of stones and throws them

after his cab, a shower of missiles that lands with a jarring rattle. The driver gives Aunty the finger and she screams more swear words and curses.

She is ferocious, A force I haven't witnessed before. We go in the house where she dishes me a bowl of vaisalo. Only then does she see my tears. She hugs me tight. An embrace of talcum powdered sweat and hands smelling of the lemons she squeezed for the morning's vai tipolo.

"Don't cry Scar. Everything will be alright. Just be a good girl." She looks over my shoulder and out the window. Mutters bad words in Samoan about kaea schools and valea teachers.

Only then do I realise that she's not angry at me. Her rage is for the school and whatever they have said to her.

That night I find out what it is.

I've been expelled. Oh they didn't use that word of course. No. They said we should think about a different school because they were worried about my influencing the other girls. Besides, didn't my parents want to get me away from the boy who had gotten me pregnant? Was he a student too? Could Aunty give them his name so the school could punish him accordingly?

"Faikala!" says Aunty with vicious disdain, scrubbing the fa'alifu pot again. Even though the umukuka cousins had already cleaned it. "Why they want to know for? Why they think you a bad girl for the other kids? You a good girl."

Mother confers with Father in his room where he holds court now from his sickbed. She comes downstairs to announce his verdict. I will go live with my great-aunts in America. My father's aunts. It will be better for the family. And for me, Mother adds as an afterthought.

It's then that Aunty does something I have never imagined she would ever do.

She disagrees with Mother.

"No. That's so far away. Let her stay."

Mother flinches as if Aunty has struck her. She launches into a tirade. Things like – how dare Filomena question the authority and wisdom of the faifeau? Who does she think she is? Has she forgotten the commandments? Children are to obey their parents that their days may be long on the earth. Is Filomena presuming to come between a child and her parents? How can a daughter who has committed sin after sin, ever repent if Filomena is going to speak this way?

Aunty doesn't back down. There is stone in her eyes and a lava rock field stretching between her and Mother.

"E le sa'o lea mea," she says. "This isn't right. Scarlet needs to be here with her aiga. Tamarina and Naomi need their big sister."

Mother brushes her words aside with a flick of her hand.

"Scarlet is going to America. That is our decision."

"If you do this thing, I'm not going to stay here anymore."

"Oh? And where will you go?" says Mother. Her lip curls. She looks at Aunty like she is a half-eaten lizard the cat has left on the kitchen floor. "O ai totogi le pili o lou uso i Mapuifagalele? Who will pay your sister's bill at the rest home? Go then. You ungrateful woman. All these years we cared for you, provided a home for you. And this is how you repay us?"

My sisters have come in to the kitchen. Quietly. Wide eyed at the frightening spectacle of the two most important women in our lives, fighting. Tamarina slips her hand into mine, and stands bone still and soundless. Never-quiet Naomi wails loudly and runs to clutch at Auntie's lavalava. She cries the words we're all screaming inside.

"Don't go Aunty! Please don't leave us." *Who will love us if you go?*

Mother is triumphant. "See girls? Aunty Filomena doesn't care about you. See how easily she decides to go from this house? Your sister has a good opportunity to live in America and go to school there, and your Aunty is being selfish." She makes an impatient sound and pulls Naomi away from Filomena. "Stop that! She is not your mother. And she doesn't even love you – she chooses Scarlet over you."

There's isupe running from Naomi's nose and she's almost not pretty as she sobs, standing beside Mother, wailing Auntie's name over and over. Pleading. "Please don't go."

Aunty tries but she is no match for Mother's iron will. There are two more daughters who need Auntie's love and Mother threatens to ban her from our home if she doesn't co-operate. And so it's decided. I will go to America. Thanks to the magic of Samoa's musty unreliable Registry office, a birth certificate is produced that declares me Great-Aunty Mareta's daughter. Never mind that it would be a Mary-Jesus miracle for a near-seventy year old woman to be the biological mother of a fourteen year old!

Aunty Filomena takes me to the airport. My sisters go too. Cousin Aukuso drives. Other boy cousins crowd into the back of the truck. Going to the airport is a sightseeing expedition. Mother stays behind to look after Father.

Naomi cries as she hugs me tight. "Why do you have to leave us?" she asks. "It's not fair Scar. You get to go to America and we have to stay here!" She is envious. "You'll get to have Barbie dolls and watch Hanna Montana all day on TV. Maybe you might see her somewhere?"

I promise her that if I meet Miley Cyrus, then I will tell her about my little sister Naomi and can she please audition to be a backup dancer at her concerts.

"Don't forget your promise Scar," says Naomi as I extricate myself from her hug.

Tamarina doesn't say anything. Just presses a lumpy package into my hands, wrapped in a piece of paper torn out of a school book. Then retreats to stand beside Cousin Aukuso.

Aunty Filomena weeps. "Be a good girl Scar. Teine lelei." She hands me over to the flight attendant who will be my escort.

When I'm sitting in my seat on the plane, then I open the package. It's our aki stones. Gleaming in their perfection. A thousand and one games cross-legged on the floor, sister squabbles, triumphant wins and dejected losses, an endless litany of laughter.

It's my sisters in the palm of my hand.

That's when I cry. Holding the stones of our childhood in my hand, wishing for one more glimpse of my family as the plane taxis down the runway.

I won't see them again for seven years.

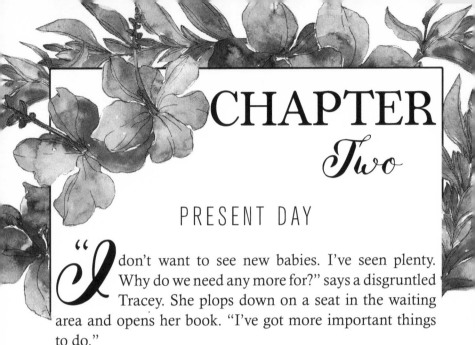

CHAPTER
Two

PRESENT DAY

"I don't want to see new babies. I've seen plenty. Why do we need any more for?" says a disgruntled Tracey. She plops down on a seat in the waiting area and opens her book. "I've got more important things to do."

I think about ordering her to go with us but decide against it. Four other child visitors is plenty. Tracey will have plenty of time to sort out her big sister issues. Hey look at me, I'm thirty and still figuring out mine.

"Aunty Scar, can we go now? I wanna see the babies," says Dana.

"Yeah, just leave her," suggests Tim, Tracey's twin and opposite in all things.

"Wanna see Mum," says Demetrius.

My stone cold heart melts a little at the sadness in his face. It's been two days since they saw their mom and an even tougher forty-eight hours for the babies. After the initial buzz of their safe delivery, baby Number Two had sent everyone into a panic when she had trouble breathing.

It had been a tense night with lots of praying from us all. She was stable now but still in an incubator and hooked up to some scary wires and beeping machines.

I'd been back and forth to the hospital ever since I first brought Tamarina in (with Jackson.) But I'm not thinking about *him*. Not now. Not ever. *Fuck Jackson.* I've put him on the shelf of THINGS I WONT THINK ABOUT, along with the earth-shattering revelations Tamarina had given me on that first night in hospital. I wasn't thinking about any of it. Father being an adulterer and cheating on Mother with her own sister. Or maybe sending me away to protect me and not because he was ashamed of me.

Nope, not thinking about any of it. See? Can't you tell?

I give myself a mental shake and return to the task at hand. Being a good Big Sister and a reliable, awesome Aunty.

Stella slips her hand in mine and tugs. "Babies, Aunty. Go see the babies." The excitement in her eyes more than makes up for Tracey's world-weary experience of being a big sister to six little siblings.

That decides it. "Tracey, you stay here, okay? Read your book. Don't go anywhere." And for good measure. "Don't do drugs. Don't drink beer. And don't talk to any boyfriends."

Tracey rolls her eyes and goes back to her book.

"Or girlfriends," adds Dana helpfully. She explains for my bemused benefit. "Mum says girls can have girlfriends too and boys can have boyfriends. You don't choose who you love."

Tim snorts. A most undignified sound. "Nobody's gonna choose Tracey anyway. She's too ugly to have a girlfriend *or* a boyfriend."

Before Tracey can volley back with an attack of her own, I herd them all down the hall. "Come on. Your mum's waiting for you. And remember, she's basically run ten marathons so be nice okay? No whinging, whining or pestering her about silly things."

In the room, Stella breaks free from my grasp and runs to hug her mother fiercely. The others follow, crowding in for their share. There's so much mother-love in the room that I have to turn away for a minute or else I'm going to break down and bawl. Must be the hormones. By association.

Stella pulls back and pats at her mother's belly with a puzzled frown. "Mama, you got another baby in there? Your tummy's still fat."

Fabulous. Just what every woman wants to hear after she's popped out twins.

Tamarina laughs though. A tired but delighted sound as she snuggles Stella close again. "Oh how I've missed you my darling!"

I'm about to say something but Demetrius gets in before me. "Don't be silly Stella. Big tummies don't always mean there's babies in it. See Aunty Scar has a fat tummy and she don't got a baby in there." He turns to me for confirmation. "Do you?"

Fabulous. Just what every fat barren aunty wants to hear.

A weary smile. "Nope. No babies in here. Just fat." I'm taking one for the team here. Distracting them all from their exhausted mother. What a noble sacrifice. (If I do say so myself.)

All of the children pause to study my belly. Intently. "How do you know for sure there's no babies in there?" asks Demetrius. His face lights up. "I saw on the Crazy Hollywood Stories program, this lady had a baby on the airplane. She didn't even know she was pregnant! She was super fat and then she had a sore stomach and BAM! Out came a baby."

Tamarina's vigilant mother radar goes off. "Who let you watch Crazy Hollywood Stories? That's not a show for children."

Oops. That would be me. Bad Aunty busted.

I am saved by the children who are still fascinated with my secret baby. Dana turns to me, excited. "Aunty Scar, you had a sore tummy yesterday. Maybe you got a baby in there! It can come out any minute." All the children are riveted on me.

"Don't be silly."

It's Tracey. She's decided to join us. With a frown, she rebukes her little sister. "Babies don't just grow from nothing. For no reason. You need to have sex with somebody first to make a baby."

Dana is immune to the rebuke. Even the word sex doesn't phase her. (But then, they do have a very progressive mother after all.) "Aunty Scar, did you have a sex with somebody?"

"Ummm what?"

"Sex," repeats Dana patiently. "Did you have any sex?"

"Aunty doesn't got a husband," says Tim primly. "You only do sex if you're married."

Tracey's scoff is enough to unsettle the dead in Sefo's Funeral parlor next door. "Can you be any dumber?! People who aren't married have sex all the time. Aunty Scar is probably having sex with a different man every week. Why should she wait until she finds a husband? Right Aunty?"

I should be pleased that my niece has so much faith in my ability to attract sex-mates. A different one every week even!

But instead, my face is on fire. Red like the teuila that I rolled around naked on in the forest a few days ago. I am sure everyone can see every scandalous fiery moment imprinted on my very being. I open my mouth and no words come out. And now my sister has a glint in her eye and she's giving me a knowing grin. Like she's put 2 + 2 together and arrived at the all-knowing, all-seeing sum of *I-know-what-you-been-doing-girl-ha.*

Damn these math geniuses. Bloody mind reader!

The excruciating moment is thankfully interrupted by a mewling sound from one of the babies.

Tamarina sighs. "Scar can you get her for me?" To the children she says firmly, "We don't ask people about their sex life. It's private and personal."

I go to get the noisemaker, carrying her with care to her weary mother. Everyone draws a little closer to get a good look as Tamarina tries to comfort the crier.

"What's wrong?" asks Stella. "What's the matter with our baby?"

"Nothing darling," soothes Tamarina. "She just wants a hug."

Now Stella is crying. Big fat tears are running down her cheeks. "She's sad. She's hurting. I don't want our baby to be sad. Please make her be okay mama."

Oh hell. We are all in for a whole lot of misery if Stella's going to have a meltdown every time one of the babies cries.

The wailing gets louder and a second voice joins in from the incubator in the corner. The children cluster around to coo soothing noises at the second baby.

"Why does she got no clothes on?" asks Demetrius? "What's that light?"

I explain that his sister has jaundice and so she needs the ultraviolet light for a while.

A nurse comes in and efficiently tends to the infant in the incubator.

"What's he doing to our baby?" asks Stella. There's a #readyToFight look on her face. "Mum he's hurting our baby!"

It takes a lot of reassuring noises and explanations, but Stella finally calms down and accepts that her sister isn't crying because she's being hurt somehow. Still, she continues to give the nurse suspicious looks from across the room and doesn't let up until he finishes his work and leaves the room.

"I don't like him," she announces. "He's got funny ears. Our baby's scared of his ears. Mama can we get a different nurse who has nice ears?"

Before her mother can reply, there's a sound at the door.

It's my brother-in-law Jacob. Rumpled, unshaven, and looking like he's travelled all night and day through several time zones to be here. Which he has.

Tracey sees him first. "Daddy!" All her big sister airs evaporate. She rushes and hugs him tight around the waist. "Mama nearly died in the car."

Jacob bends to hug her back, whispering reassurance, but all the while his eyes don't waver from his wife. In that gaze is an endless ocean of love, hope and worry. Quick hugs for the other children and then he crosses the room in several long strides to take Tamarina in his arms. Towering tall, broad and built like a prop rugby player, he is a force of restrained strength and as I stand there, I see my forever calm and unruffled genius little sister crumple.

"I was so scared," she whispers. "I needed you." And finally, after how many days of tension and fear, she bursts into tears.

Jacob holds her in a soothing embrace. "I'm sorry." He's a man of few words. Even now. "I'm proud of you," he says in his distinctive deep timbre voice. "You did good."

They are oblivious to us all. Babies, sisters, children, nurse and all. Secure in their world that can't be shaken or stirred so long as they are together.

I want to take a photo and log it under the dictionary definition of love. Then I want to cry too. Because they're beautiful. And also because I had a fight with Jackson and now I'll never have a Hallmark card moment with him like this one. I shake off the self-pity and rouse myself back to Aunty duties., ushering the children out of there and shushing their complaints.

"No let's leave them to have a bit of space to themselves, okay?"

Stella is indignant, "Mummies and Dada's don't want space to themselves. Why did they have us for then?"

I soothe her and try bribery. "We're going to get ice cream. Double scoops for everyone to celebrate the new babies."

They don't want to go, but I make them, throwing one more glance back over their shoulders at their parents lost in an embrace that encompasses every missed minute and frantic fragile breath over the last two days.

For a moment I am stabbed all over with envy, coveting this. The love in the room. The steadfastness and the surety. *Will I ever find that? Will that ever be me?*

CHAPTER
Three

JACKSON

*W*hen she wasn't making me laugh, Scarlet was making me mad. And through the two extremes, she made me hard. How is it possible for one person to make me feel so many wildly different things, and usually all within the space of a few minutes?

Take that night of the wedding for an example. Sitting across the room at the table with the other bridesmaids, she was a vision of luscious beauty that I couldn't tear my eyes away from her. That dress was scandalous the way it cradled her breasts in a scarlet wrapped offering that threatened to break free at any minute. The disapproving looks from every senior Aunty who passed by had me grinning. But the lascivious stares of every unrelated male in the room made me grit my teeth and clench my fists. I wanted to break their necks. Or at least forcibly remove them from the reception. She was dancing with one of them now and he was trying to get up in her personal space even though it was a fast Enrique Iglesias number and there was no reason for him to be trying to put his paws on her waist.

My irritation must have shown because Troy had nudged me, "Hey, you okay? You look like the French team all walked in, and we're down by three all over again."

I had to laugh at the rush of memory he'd evoked. We had both been typecast in college, pushed towards playing basketball. Troy even more so. In rebellion we had signed up for the whitest sport we could find – water polo – and then worked like hell to excel. It had given us great satisfaction to be eventually selected for the US Olympic team and losing to France in the final still rankled. It may have been over ten years ago but I still didn't like telling people about my water polo past. A silver medal meant that we'd lost and I hated that.

Troy was waiting for my response and his grin had faded, replaced by a raised eyebrow and a thoughtful look. He was way too astute and the only reason he hadn't picked up on my thing with Scarlet, was because of the wedding chaos. But he had given me that look. The one that said, *I know something's up and you better spill. Or else.*

"Don't worry about me, old man. You've got more pressing concerns now." I waved to a flock of senior relatives who were dancing in a wild circle. "Aunty, Troy wants to join you. Can you teach him some of your siva moves?"

They hadn't needed any more encouragement and Troy was quickly borne to the dance floor. He'd thrown me a murderous look as he went and I laughed.

Once he was out of the way, I'd gone back to watching Scarlet. She'd finished dancing with the creep and was back at the table, eating with gusto. Where the other bridesmaids politely picked at their food, Scarlet savoured each bite, eating with the same intensity as when she made love. With complete and utter sensory enjoyment. She popped a mussel into her mouth and half-closed her eyes as she licked the curry coconut cream off her fingers. I flashed back to that day on the plane, watching her eat savouries like they were manna from heaven, and just like that day, I was immediately, uncomfortably hard.

This is messed up. Who gets a hard-on simply from watching their lover eat seafood? From across the other side of a crowded room?

I couldn't tear my eyes away from her.

Then Scarlet stood up and waved to one of the waiters. Obviously another one of her cousins as he smiled and – in response to her request – handed over not one, but two of the petite bowls of dessert. There was an untouched dessert serving in front of me and I wanted to go over and take her mine so she could smile at me like that. So I could sit beside her and feed her, so I could alternate custard trifle with kisses.

I'd wanted her so bad, I could taste it. All I wanted was to take her away from there. Back to my hotel. Where I would finally get to have her all to myself. Cars, forests and church supply rooms became magic when Scarlet was in them, but a bed? And a lock on the door? With none of her 101 relatives around to disturb us? It would be heaven.

Then the baby emergency happened. And it was pretty

special – although not quite the night I had been hoping for. Seeing another side of Scarlet, her panicked vulnerability and how much she cared for her sister had brought out a protective instinct in me that I didn't know I had. And when her mother had blasted her like that? I hated seeing Scarlet wither and retreat inside herself. I kept seeing it when she was around her family. Like a glorious flower wilting.

And for what? For people who treated her like shit? Even now, remembering the scene in the hospital waiting room had me clenching my fists. I had my fair share of shit mother experiences but Mrs Thompson was in a whole other sphere of fucked-up.

But I had overstepped. Scarlet wasn't mine to protect. She wasn't mine to shelter. Something she'd pointed out to me. She was right. She wasn't mine.

But I wanted her to be.

How had this happened? In the space of only a few weeks, this woman with her rich belly laugh, wicked sense of humour, and the most glorious body I'd ever seen - had become the person I thought about when I first wake up. It's her face I see in the heated dreams I'd been having since arriving. It's the sound of her laugh that I follow in a crowded room. How did this happen?

When she said this was just a holiday buzz fling – it had been like a boot to the gut. Because I wanted more of this woman.

But now thanks to my big mouth, my inability to stay out of her family drama, I may have ruined any chance to make this more than a holiday fling. I was supposed to fly out in a few more days. I had to fix this. Quick. But how?

CHAPTER
Four

SCARLET

Now that Jacob is here, I can ease up on Big Sister duties. Which makes me an easy target for the Aunties. Because all the baggage that goes with the wedding of the year still hasn't finished. Naomi and Troy are back from spending two honeymoon nights at a resort on the other side of the island and now we can open the wedding presents. As in, the entire extended family aiga. As in, all six hundred plus presents. Just as the aiga had planned, actioned and paid for the wedding, so too must they share in the wedding bounty as well.

The big fale had to be set up appropriately and food prepared. Large steaming vats of chop suey and stir fry. A couple of pigs roasted. Siaosi and his crew of boy cousins had been up most of the night prepping everything for the umu. Aunty Filomena had made her signature puligi's and was letting me make the custard to go with them.

Aunty Valerie was not happy that Troy's parents had already gone back to America, flying away on their private jet. I could only imagine their bemusement when invited to attend the opening of the wedding presents.

"Can you believe it?" Aunty Valerie snaps, from her

chair at the front of the fale where she sits supervising the preparations. "She say no that's alright, they don't need to know anything about the mealofa's! So rude. What? They think they too rich to accept any presents? They too good for this aiga?"

She pauses in her tirade to yell at a passing boy cousin and jab at him with her walking stick. "Vale! Stupid! Don't walk on the fala? See your dirty feet? Amio pua'a."

The cousin winces and leaps nimbly out of her reach, taking his accused pig-feet back outside the fale.

Mother rushes to soothe her sister. "It's not that Valerie. Troy's parents are very busy. The Senator has to go back to do her important government work. They were here for a week you know. That's a long time to be away from her position."

It's clear from Valerie's grim expression that she doesn't think that's an acceptable excuse.

Both women are thankfully distracted by the truck pulling up to the side of the fale. It's full of wrapped gifts stacked high and everyone under the age of 30 is called to come and help unload them. There's too many to fit on the tables we have lined up and so others are carefully stacked behind them. A second truck of gifts will have to wait.

There's something about pretty presents wrapped in pretty paper that eases the tension of the rushed morning and soon there's a festive feeling as everyone works.

Someone turns the radio up and we are moving in synch to the music, with some singing and humming. Then Cousin Siaosi breaks into an impromptu siva and several old Aunties jump to join him. Anyone who's seen old Samoan women dancing to a Samoan-style remake of a hip hop song will know what I mean when I say – the party had well and truly begun. The older the aunty, the wilder their dance moves, and soon their antics had the rest of us cheering and urging them on with often graphic half-insults and encouragement.

I pause to watch, stepping outside the scene with my writer's detachment, and a sudden burst of happiness catches me by surprise.

This, this is what home is. All the bitching aside, this is Samoa, this is aiga. A woman in her sixties, wearing a orange floral mu'umu'u, dancing in a near-obscene fashion with one of the fale posts. Another having a Gangnam dance contest with one of my teenage cousins – and he's clearly losing. I'm surrounded by family, laughter, music and wild dancing. My sister and her babies are okay. Her husband made it safe to be by her side. My other sister is married to the love of her life (for now anyway). And I know there's a big platter of faausi in the kitchen, waiting for dessert time. For a moment, just a moment – I know this is joy.

Of course it doesn't last. *Eh.*

One of the cousins trips mid dance step as he's transporting a present inside the fale. The tinkling crash of something precious shattering makes a spectacular noise and just like that, the party's over.

Aunty Valerie launches into a tirade filled with too many curse words to write them all. (I'm not sure I even know how to spell them...) The music is switched off, and everyone is told to get back to work. The bashed present is opened by the senior aunties and more cursing eventuates when they see it's a box of wine glasses.

Then Mother catches sight of me. "Scar look at you! Go kaele and get ready. Everyone will be here soon."

I deep sigh as I go back inside the house like an #ObedientDaughter. But my annoyance with her is tempered somewhat because now I know the truth. Can I ever see my mother and her twin the same way, now that I know? For a strange moment I want to hug Mother. I think about how it would feel if my sister slept with my husband. Of course I don't have a husband, but IF I had one....*who looks like Jackson Emory...who IS Jackson Emory.* A surge of rage. I would beat my sister to a pulp if that were me. And quite possibly chop my imaginary husband into a hundred imaginary little pieces.

Unbidden, an image of Jackson comes to mind. Of us. Bodies entwined. I shiver in the humidity and then force myself back to reality. Me and Jackson are not together. We are not a 'thing'. And thanks to our argument, there will be no more ecstatic encounters of any kind. In the bushes or anywhere else. The end.

It's time for the present unwrapping. A car pulls up. It's Naomi and Troy. My sister is flushed and happy, even prettier in her post honeymoon glow, blushing prettily as cousins tease her about honeymoon sexy-times. Because of course the only acceptable script here is that she was a nervous virgin being gently instructed in the arts of all things sexual by her masterful husband.

I'm feeling magnanimous though so I don't think any mean spiteful thoughts. *Nah* I put them into storage for another time when Naomi is being bitchy and deserves them.

Like a dutiful eldest daughter, I am wearing the hideous puletasi Mother had made for me. The satin peach one with gigantic white lace flowers sewed on to it. The one that sticks and clings in all the wrong places – like my belly. But is a voluminous sack where my boobs are. Because heaven help us all if anyone knows I have breasts. It's the ugliest puletasi ever invented. Even though I just showered, there's already giant sweat stains around my armpits and the satin is sticking to me in suspiciously wet patches.

I am fussing with the lavalava trying to make it look slightly less ugly when a rental car pulls up in front. It's Jackson. Oh shit.

"Why is he here for?" I hiss at Naomi as Troy goes out to meet him.

I haven't seen him or heard from him since that night at the hospital. Two very long days. I thought he had gone back to America and just the thought of that made me sick and sad. Sick and sad enough that I'd been drowning my sad sick sorrows in wedding leftovers.

She gives me a surprised look. "Because he's the best man stupid! Why wouldn't he be here?"

"The wedding is finished. He's not needed any more. Shouldn't he be flying back to America? Doesn't he have a business to run?" I say grumpily.

"He's the CEO of a billion dollar company. I think he can do whatever he wants," she retorts. "Besides, what's it to you? Why are you being so mean anyway? I thought he'd been very nice to you. Considering."

My eyes narrow. "Considering what?" Hands on my hips. "Considering that I'm a fat bucket?"

"No you egg. Considering how bitchy you've been to him from day one. You're always snapping at him and being rude. I don't know why he even still talks to you." Naomi flounces away with an eye roll. "Excuse me, I have presents to open."

I look across the yard to where Jackson is standing with Troy beside the fale. The two are smiling and talking easily. But as if he can sense my gaze, Jackson turns and before I can look away and pretend to be very busy with something else, anything else – our eyes meet. Catch.

And I am lost. Incredibly, desperately, breathtakingly lost.

How is it possible that I have fallen so far and so fast for this man who only entered my life – via airplane – a mere few weeks ago? This can't be right. This can't be happening to me. It's not fair. It's not possible.

He looks at me like he knows me, like he sees me. All the ragged scattered pieces of me – and makes sense of them. All the rage that smoulders within me – and understands it.

It's a shared gaze that could be a moment or an eternity, I'm not sure. Interrupted only when Mother jerks at the sleeve of my puletasi and pulls me back to the present and the swirling bustle of activity.

"Scar! Hurry up. It's time to start."

It's wedding present show time.

In the fale, I go to sit beside the table, wincing at the awkward discomfort of sitting cross-legged. It's been a long time since we had to sit like this for hours at school during assemblies and culture dance practises. But asking for a chair will tell everyone that I'm one of those useless Samoans from overseas who can't sit on the floor properly. So even though I *am* one of those useless Samoans from overseas, I grin and bear it. I sneak a glance over at Jackson who's next to Troy. The aunties have given him a lavalava to cover up his shorts and it gives me a grim satisfaction to see him struggle for a few minutes to fuss with the tying and wrapping and then awkwardly try to figure out how to sit cross-legged with a lavalava on.

Ha. You useless palagi.

It doesn't make me feel better to insult him though. I remember his words to me at the hospital and I'm trying to get mad at him all over again, but now in the honest light of a new day – they don't seem that bad anymore. In the light of everything Tamarina revealed to me about my parents, things that I have yet to process, it doesn't seem so bad for Jackson to tell me that I need to break free of my family? Was he really so wrong to say those things? Because if I'm being honest with myself, weren't there some grains of truth in them?

In the festive air of the wedding present fale, I admit it to myself. I'm tired of swallowing the nonu leaf bitterness that my family dishes out. Will I ever be old enough, independent enough, strong enough – to speak my truth? To put up barriers against their shit?

"Scarlet are you going to help or not?" asks a petulant Lucia.

Seeing her reminds me with a jolt that she knows things that could get me in trouble. What if she tells my aunties about seeing me with Jackson? I give myself a mental shake. Because so what if she does? I give her a sickly sweet smile and say with my best breathy skank voice, "Oh sorry Lucia. I'm a little distracted. Jackson has me all tired out. He can't keep his hands off me!"

She narrows her perfectly accented eyes at me and flounces away to sit beside the other bridesmaids.

Yes I'm petty. So shoot me.

The gift-opening begins. This is where the usefulness of having twenty million bridesmaids finally makes itself known. We have to unwrap each beribboned box, and hold it up so everyone can see it as we announce the name of the gift-giver. I feel like one of those chicks carrying the Round notice card at a boxing match. Except of course, minus the high heels and glossy blonde hair. And plus a hundred pounds and a voluminous satin puletasi. (*Minor details ha…*) The gathered crowd nods their heads appreciatively, sometimes they break into applause at a particularly fabulous present. Like the microwave from the faifeau. And the Plantation House bedspread set with pillows from Naomi's office team.

Once we have unwrapped and displayed each gift, then it's time for the sharing.

One by one, each senior member of the aiga gets a gift from the assorted feast of offerings. Aunty Valerie is in charge of the divvying up of presents. She points with her stick and we bridesmaids must leap to do her bidding. There are four rice cookers and Aunty Valelia designates the biggest and most shiniest is for the faifeau's wife. I go to carry it and nearly tear something important in my back as I try to heft and heave the box up off the cement floor. There's a titter of laughter and I think bad words about my kaea family who – typical Samoan style - would rather sit and laugh at me first, rather than jumping to help me carry this monstrosity.

And then he is there. Jackson. Strong hands take the box from me. A macadamia honey voice says, "I got it."

I straighten up, still holding on to the box. Because I'm stubborn. *I can carry it! I'm strong enough!* For a moment we face each other across a cardboard box, me sweaty and huffing out of breath. Him, cool and calm and giving me that look I could drown in. Staring down at me, with eyes I could get lost in. He's not smiling. But there's a softness in his eyes. Like there's words he wants to say. Words like...

I don't care about your weird family Scar...I still want you...I adore you! I can't live without you! In fact, I just realised, I love you! Let's run away into the sunset together!

Of course he doesn't say any of that.

Yes, I have a wild imagination. I write romance novels remember?

Whatever words he's really thinking, whatever feelings he's really feeling – they are abruptly interrupted by Aunty Valerie reaching out with her walking stick to jab me in the backside.

"Hurry up! E ke valea? Are you stupid?"

Good old Aunty. I grit my teeth in a smile for her and the waiting crowd. Everything is a performance in faaSamoa after all. Jackson raises an eyebrow at me in question, but I give him a barely discernible shake of my head. *It's all good Jackson from America. This is normal Samoan family stuff. How we show our love for each other.* I let him carry the box by himself to where the pastor's wife is waiting for her share of the bounty. Jackson makes the presentation the way he's seen us do it, with a bow and an exaggerated show of humility, like we the gift-givers are incredibly blessed and lucky to be able to give gifts to our betters.

I may have ogled his backside as he did the bowing and scraping. Just for a moment. Because how can anyone with eyes **not** admire all of that fine-ness?

I go back to stand with the other bridesmaids and Malia, one of the nicer girls nudges me and whispers dramatically, "What was that Scarlet?!"

"What's what?" I mutter out of the side of my mouth. All the aunties can see us up here. So can my crocodile of a mother.

"The way he was staring at you. See? He's doing it again!" she says, vibrant with restrained excitement.

I look at Jackson, and Malia is right. He's staring at me. A deeply intense, overwhelming gaze, like he's thinking about how he can devour me. Savour me. 101 different ways. It's the most erotic thing I've ever seen and I suddenly feel faint in this crowded fale.

"I need some water," I mumble, and stumble out of the fale. I don't have to look at her to know Mother is annoyed at my exit.

Chill Mother. There's nineteen other bridesmaids. I'm sure the show will go on.

Cousin Siaosi is outside by the food tent, fanning flies and taking selfies on his phone.

"What's wrong sis?" he asks, concerned. "You drink too much last night?"

Without waiting for a reply, he gets me a plastic chair to sit on, and a cup of lukewarm vai tipolo.

"I gotchu," he says generously as he waves me with his fan.

"Can I ask your advice?"

The ceremony is ongoing and everyone in the fale is fixated on the presents. Nobody is paying attention to me and Siaosi. I can't see Jackson from this spot. Good. Looking at him makes my brain a mess.

"Ask me anything cuz," says Siaosi. "I'm here for you."

He has an earnest look on his face. My cousin is totally committed to being my confidante right now, to giving me advice. I shove aside the voice of caution that says – *what the hell does a 23yr old who's perpetual happiness is marijuana-induced know about relationships?! Or about matters of the heart?*

But I take a deep breath and ask anyway. Because what do I have to lose? Who else am I going to ask?

"How do you know that a man really cares about you? Like, really cares for you and wants to be with you?"

If Siaosi is surprised that I'm asking him about men, he doesn't show it. No, he assumes a sage expression and nods knowingly.

"Ah yes, that's an important question. How long have you known this man?"

Suddenly remembering that Siaosi is one of the biggest faikala gossips in the whole family, I rush to put some qualifiers into the question.

"Oh it's not me. I'm asking for a friend."

Siaosi isn't convinced. "A friend huh?"

"Yes. A friend. She needs some advice and I told her I would ask my cousin who's experienced in these things."

I'm not sure he believes me on "the friend" bit, but he does like the compliment.

He preens. "Yes well I am very experienced. But that's what happens when so many girls want me. You know even Analosa the pastor's daughter, keeps texting me. Oka, I tell you, you wouldn't even believe she's a faifeau's daughter! Look at this..."

He shows me a text that I wish I hadn't seen. A message that makes me want to wash my brain out with disinfectant.

"Siaosi! I didn't want to see that. Really!?"

He shrugs. "What? I told you, it's not my fault. She's the one messaging me all the time. All the day. All the night. That girl really wants me."

We are getting distracted here. I don't want to talk about Analosa. I now never want to see Analosa again either. Can we get back to my question? My problem?

"Okay. But what about when you like a girl. What do you do? How do you show her that you really want her. You really care about her."

Siaosi considers my question for a minute. "Do you mean, if I want to do the sex with her? Or if I want to marry her?"

I splutter. "Is there a difference?"

"Of course. A man can want to do sex with lots of different women. Doesn't mean he wants his friends to know about her. Or his family."

"That's not very nice," I say hotly. I didn't know my favorite boy cousin was such a shit.

"Yes it is. It's for her protection. Think about it. You know my sisters. Why would I let them meet every girl I have sex with? Sita and Lina are like the devil. Any girl I go with, if they know about them, they will treat them so bad. Maybe try to fasi them. That's not fair on the girls. No," he shakes his head vehemently. "Only until I decide to get married, then I will let my family meet the girl. Because

61

then I can protect her and she will be my wife and I can try to make my devil sisters be nice."

He looks rather glum then. Probably thinking about his devil sisters. I look over to the fale where Sita and Lina are sitting, cheering and laughing with the others as new gifts are given out. They look harmless enough but Siaosi's right. If they knew what was on his phone from Analosa? They would take it upon themselves to teach her how a good Bible-abiding girl should behave...

This is going to be more difficult than I thought, the cultural context is different!

"How about if the man is not Samoan?"

Siaosi immediately wrinkles his nose. Ugh. "He's palagi?"

"Yes. My friend likes a palagi."

"And your friend is Samoan?" Siaosi really doesn't like this. Anyone would think from his expression that I was proposing a union between two different species.

"What's wrong?" I demand, with a nod to the fale. "Troy's not Samoan and you like him for Naomi."

"That's different. He came here and lived with Samoans. He knows our ways. And he's meauli."

I wince. "Tama uli. Black man. Not black thing."

Siaosi shrugs, *whatever*. "Troy is not palagi. It's different. And he knows our ways."

"Alright fine. Let's say my friend likes a palagi who knows our ways. How can she tell if he cares about her?"

I'm starting to wish I hadn't asked Siaosi anything. Not only is this a frustrating conversation, he's also giving me that look. The one that says, *'I'm not stupid. I know you got no friends. You've been banging a palagi and now you're freaking out…'*

Siaosi purses his lips like the judgey twenty-three year old that he is and says, "Your friend will know he cares if he follows her everywhere."

"You mean, he stalks her?" I am doubtful.

Siaosi is confident in his wisdom. A nod. "Yes. He goes everywhere she goes. Did you watch that vampire movie where he sits in the tree outside her bedroom every night? That's how you know a palagi likes you. Samoans don't do that. Only if you're a moekolo and what girl wants a boy like that? We fasi moekolo's if we catch them."

He's not finished. "He will buy her presents. And give her flowers. But not ones you pick from the pa aute hedge outside. He will get her flowers you have to buy from a shop."

I think of making love in a bed of red teuila, emerald leaves and golden mosooi…and my face flushes as the day suddenly gets hotter.

Siaosi is really getting into this. I can see he's put a lot of thought into palagi's and their romance ways, vs Samoans and their intricacies. I'm storing all this info away in my romance author archives.

"Samoan boys don't give girls flowers then?" I tease his theory.

But he is confidently certain. "Flowers?" A snort of derision. "No. Why would she want useless things like that? They're growing everywhere. No. A Samoan girl wants food. You take her somewhere nice to eat. Analosa likes the lunch at Pinati's."

I raise an eyebrow at him. "Oh really? I thought you weren't interested in her? That she was sending you dirty messages because she admires your dirty nasty self from a distance?"

He has the grace to look sheepish. "Maybe I like her a little bit."

I think about Jackson bringing me misiluki pudding from Paddles. That counts as buying me nice things that I like, right?

Siaosi continues. "He will buy things for her family too. He will know that her family is very important and so he will give them presents too."

We both look at the gleaming silver car in the driveway. The one that announces proudly that my sister's husband loves and respects her parents.

"Anything else? What about if he always wants to lick…" Wait up, this is my boy cousin. We can't talk about sex with details. "What about if he always wants to *be* with her. In a physical way. Surely that's a sign that he wants her?"

Siaosi looks disgusted. "No! He won't do any sex with her. Even if he wants to. He will know that her brothers and cousins will fasi him if he touches her. We will send him to the hospital."

Now this is just silly. What did Siaosi think Troy and Naomi were doing all year before they got married? I'm about to ask him exactly that question but then I shut my mouth again. Because Naomi's sex life is none of my business. And it's certainly none of Siaosi's business either.

It's Siaosi's turn to ask a question. "Did your friend already do the sex with this palagi?"

This is a minefield. Is Siaosi going to leap up and start smashing people?

"Umm, maybe. I'm not sure. She didn't tell me everything."

Siaosi casual demeanour is gone now, replaced by the most serious version of my cousin that I've ever seen. He glances at the fale to make sure nobody is eavesdropping, and then lowers his voice.

"Tell your friend she must be careful. Some palagi are no good. They only want to use you. They think Samoans are easily available. That they can buy you. Or impress you with their palagi ways. I have met palagi women who treat us like that."

He pauses and in that hesitation I sense shame.

"What is it Siaosi? Tell me."

"No. It is not good for a boy to tell his sister such things. But just know that some palagi don't treat Samoans as equals. They might tell you nice words, buy you gifts and even get in a relationship with you, but you are never on the same level as them. Be careful Scar."

In that moment there is no pretence between us. He knows what I am asking and I know he is gifting me a vulnerable part of himself. "Troy is special," he adds. "I was suspicious of him at first, but then I watched and I see how he treats your sister. I see he loves her more than himself. I see he always holds her up high. Then I know he is real. He is true."

"So you didn't ever have to fasi him," I joke lightly, wanting to break the tense secrecy between us.

Siaosi laughs. "No fasi for Troy!" But he's not ready to stop being serious. Not yet. "Troy's friend - Jackson seems like a nice man. Maybe he is different. But it's too soon to know. Too early to tell. Be careful."

My cousin has stunned me. He knows about Jackson? How? I haven't given Siaosi enough credit, dismissing him as a happy-go-lucky ganja-smoker. Before I can quiz him on the topic of Jackson, my mother calls from the fale.

"Bring vai tipolo for the guests. Hurry!"

And just like that my relationship advice session with the wise Siaosi is finished. I scurry back to bridesmaid duties but mulling over his words. *Some palagi look down to Samoans. We are not the same as them. We are not equal. Be careful.*

I don't get any more opportunities to stare into Jackson's eyes. Or to imagine all his imaginary declarations of love for me. Which is probably for the best.

COUSIN SIAOSI'S ADVICE
WHEN A PALAGI DATES A SAMOAN

The first thing you must remember is that Samoans don't date. Ask any Samoan about this thing called 'dating' and they will laugh in your face. All your relatives are your cousins. Anyone not related to you, is your friend and you can't go anywhere with your friend unless your cousins go too. We don't date. Not the way palagi's do anyway.

The second thing you have to know is a Samoan woman can't ever openly say that she's attracted to someone. Or interested in them at all. Even if Jason Momoa or Sonny Bill Williams knocked on her family's door? She would have to say no thank you and please go away right now. If any of her aunties or cousins are watching, then she will probably even get a salu to sweep him out the door. And throw rocks at him as he runs fast down the road. (But making sure to have bad aim because nobody would want to risk scarring their beauty. Of course.) She would have to do the same if it were the son of the faifeau. Or a man who just won the Lotto.

That's because, like I said, Samoans don't date. Not officially. And remember, there's officially only two kinds of woman.

First, you are a good Christian girl who never has sex, isn't interested in sex (not even with Jason Momoa), but always prays and goes to church, and works hard to serve her family. Then suddenly, you are getting married and ready to be a good wife. How did you find that husband? The official story is that you prayed a lot to Jesus and He sent him to you. No dating. But unofficially? Behind the pa auke scenes, you sent a message to Jason to please forgive you for throwing stones at him and to please meet you at the church youth meeting tonight where you will exchange hot lustful looks at each other from across the hall. Then you will sneak out and meet him at the Marina where you will dance and drink and possibly engage in lustful acts. But 'date' him? No.

The second kind of woman is a pa'umuku. A slut. She doesn't care about the rules or about what people think. She goes on dates and probably has sex in the bushes with every one of them. Then she either gets pregnant or she causes fights and great upheaval in the aiga. She never finds a good husband and she is a source of immense shame to her family, and constant gossip for everyone else. Officially, nobody wants to be this kind of woman.

So if you are a palagi man and you like a Samoan woman, then you have to be smart about it. You have to know the culture. The ways of our people. How do you do it? How do you get to know that pretty girl and make her family love you? You follow these steps.

Be friends with her brothers. This is very important. Her brothers can kill you. Or they can drink Taula beer with you and be happy. If you make them your friends first before you try anything with their sister, then if they need to fasi you, they'll hold back and they'll have bad aim when they throw rocks at you. Since you can't go out on dates with the woman you like, the best way to spend time with her, is to spend time with her family.

Which leads to number two. Be a servant. In Samoa, we have a special word — faiava. It means, man who comes into woman's family and is next to dirt. Just kidding. It means man who comes into woman's family and so he has no voice, no rights, no nothing. There, doesn't that sound better?!

When you are at the woman's family, you must make yourself useful. Do the feau's. Always go to the kitchen, never sit in the living room. Even better, go to the outside umukuka where the cooking boys are and help them with the firewood and to valu the popo. Help make the umu and the saka. You could be the CEO of your own company, or the Captain of the All Blacks rugby team, but if you don't know how to do chores and recognise that your place is at the bottom of the family feau's chart, then you're doomed. You may get the girl but her family will forever be stabbing you in the back and loudly mocking your uselessness to everyone they know. Samoans may be impressed by money and prestige, but if you want our lasting respect? Then understand that above all else, we value service.

1.   Be nice to her grandma, to her aunties, to her mother, to her great-grandma. But never look at her sisters. Stare at the ground. Don't smile at them. Don't laugh with them. Don't share food with them. You can be friends with her brothers but stay away from her sisters. In Samoa, the line between brother and sister is very clear. Don't make the mistake of being friendly to her sisters.

2.   Always take your shoes off before you come inside the house. Or else we will know you are dirty. Who wants a dirty man for their daughter? And I have to say it – make sure you kaele before you visit. I say that because I have noticed some palagi's have different ideas of what clean means. We shower in the morning and the night. We shower after rugby practise. We shower before we go to church. We shower before we go to Bingo. My palagi friends say that sometimes they 'forget' to kaele. For several days at a time. What kind of person FORGETS

to kaele?! How is that even possible?

3.   Always bring food when you visit. Bring food on Saturday for the lunch. Bring food on Sunday for toonai. Bring food to birthdays, parties, funerals and baptisms. But never bring a salad. That's not real food. That's just asking for our disdain. And portions are very important. If there's five people in her family, never bring a dish with only five servings on it. That's a sure sign that you are the worst kind of palagi. Siu and le mafaufau. Cheap and you have no brains. For example, a good way to casually drop by on a Sunday evening? Bring ten loaves of hot fresh bread from Siaosi's bakery and a tray of coconut buns to have with koko. That way you are acknowledging the existence of not only her parents and brothers and sisters, but also her grandparents, her aunties and uncles that may be visiting, and any cousins that are working in the umukuka.

4.   If you really want to go big, then bring a Size Two roast pig. And a basket of umu kalo and palusami. Plates from Treasure Garden are also acceptable. Not the cheap plates with too many vegetables. No. The sweet and sour pork. Lemon chicken. The whole fish in black bean sauce. And egg foo yong. Combination noodles. Other events require a box of herrings or a pusa moa. A five pound corned beef pisupo. Remember, when you date a Samoan girl, you are dating her family. Which means feed her family.

5.   No public displays of affection. Don't touch her. Ever. So what if you've been visiting her family for a whole

year now? So what if her grandmother calls you her son, and her father lets you watch wrestling on the TV with him? Men and women who are dating #notDating, don't touch. It's good if you ignore her most of the time when you come over to visit. Everyone in the aiga knows that you're there to see their daughter, but we will all pretend that you aren't. And if you ruin the fantasy by trying to hold her hand or compliment her? Then we will be forced to throw you out. And fasi you.

Good luck!

CHAPTER
Five

JACKSON

*T*he longer I stay in Samoa, the more I'm learning. Take today for example. The wedding present extravaganza was supposed to be a complication-free event. As explained by Naomi to Troy who then explained it to me. I quite liked the sound of it actually. The wedding presents would be opened publicly and witnessed by all the family, and then key members of the family would be allocated gifts. I guess when you have 600 guests, no wedding gift registry and multiple copies of the same thing, it made sense to share the abundance with your family. Especially since they'd all helped with the wedding and contributed so much to the new couple.

The more I learn about Samoan traditions, the more I'm learning about Scarlet, and the more I'm coming to understand how difficult it is to separate a person from her family in any way. So for me to hassle her about stepping away from her family's judgement and not care so much about what they wanted for her, what they think of her? Was stupid of me. How could she break free from her family when they were an intrinsic part of her?

I was pushing it staying on so this long. The office was on my case. There were projects that needed me on them and Rex my PA was getting testy during our daily phone calls.

"You were only supposed to be gone for two weeks sir," he said in a particularly aggrieved voice this morning.

"Things have come up," I said in what I hoped was a soothing tone. Rex had a tendency to freak out when everything wasn't perfectly controlled. He was a micromanager, which made him effective at his job, and made my life much easier. And usually I was more than happy and ready to carry my share of the workload. Because I loved my work and had a tendency to work too hard and too long. Something my ex had always hated and a reason why she eventually broke up with me.

"Rex, I know you have everything under control there. Give me a few more days. I have something important to settle here."

"Oh a construction project for us perhaps sir?" His business radar pinged eagerly at the thought that maybe I was staying on in Samoa to drum up business for the company.

"Not that kind of project. It's personal." My tone left no room for further argument and Rex backed off.

"Of course sir. Everything is fine here," he said smoothly.

I had bought myself a few more days, but for what? I need to breach this distance between Scarlet and I, but how? And what exactly was I hoping for?

CHAPTER
Six

SCARLET

The next day we are up early to make a mad dash for the ferry to Savaii. We are doing a wedding party pilgrimage to go see my Grandmother's sister. Great-Aunty Pativaine is the matriarch of my mother's aiga. Too frail to make the journey to Apia for the wedding, but strong enough to demand we seek an audience with her so she can 'bless' the wedding union. Or else curses will rain down upon us all no doubt. You don't mess with the elders. Especially not when they're as old as Aunty Pativaine. She doesn't know how old she is exactly. Could be ninety-nine. Or a hundred and ten. What is certain is that she has a mind as sharp as a shiny new sapelu, and that means she has an accumulated arsenal of legacy power and genealogy knowledge. You can't argue with someone who's been alive as long as she has and her testimony about lineage has literally made and broken matai chiefly title holders across the country. If she says your grandfather lied about how he got his claim to a title? And there's nobody else left alive to contradict her? Then the Lands and Titles court will cede to her every time. Knowledge is power and in a country with communal land ownership, Aunty Pativaine's family history knowledge reigned supreme.

Aunty Pativaine is also responsible for the Savaii

delegation gown that Naomi wore briefly at the reception. We are taking it with us on this pilgrimage so that she can wear it when we see Aunty. To do otherwise would be a gratuitous insult, not to mention, really stupid. Naomi may be a very model of a modern Samoan woman, but even she doesn't turn her nose up at the power and authority of a matriarch. There's always been whispers that Aunty Pativaine is in cahoots with Teine Sa. Or that she used to be one herself, a spiritual healer and bearer of curses.

The ferry ride is glorious. The sunrise is breath-taking and there's dolphins dancing along the side of the boat, splashing in the lacy surf wake. I stand by the railing, watching Upolu fall away behind us and with it, a growing lightness within, like all the upheaval and emotional stress of the last few weeks is being left behind.

Salelologa is busy and dusty as usual. A small child is selling niu and she bestows me with a gleeful smile as I buy an entire basket. She gets another coconut from a different basket and adds it to mine, "A present for you!"

But her smile quickly turns to suspicious disgust as she finds an American coin amongst the handful I have handed over to her.

"E le kaulia le kupe lea!" This money is no good here. Useless!

A cluster of children gather round for added moral support, all lacerating me with disdainful looks and mutterings about how *rich Samoans from overseas come here and try to rip off poor children in Savaii!*

I fumble through my purse, apologising profusely, looking for more coins. Why is it that when you need them – then you can't find any? "I'm sorry. It was an accident. I promise. I didn't do it on purpose."

Yeah right you plastic Samoan.

Sweat soaks my shirt as I take back the coins and hand over a $50 tala note. "Do you have any change?"

Ha. Of course not. She is glaring at me. This tiny fierce niu warrior for social justice looking like she might beat me up because I just tried to con her with a quarter.

Oh what the hell. "Take it all. Keep the change. And again, I'm sorry about the wrong money."

She grabs the money but is not appeased. Before I can carry my basket and hustle away from there, she reaches in and takes out the bonus coconut. *No meaalofa for you!*

Are you for real little girl? Really? I apologised and gave you fifty tala for fuck's sake. I don't like you. I don't like any of you niu brats.

I lug the basket back to the truck where Beyonce is laughing uproariously at my shame.

"You could stop laughing and come help me carry this, y'know," I say.

But she only laughs at me more from the air conditioning.

I am determined to sulk all the way to our mother's village but Savaii is too beautiful to fester and brood. It's been too long since I came to the big island and the scenery along the ribbon curves of road quickly soothes and embraces. There's no ocean quite as blue and sparkling clear as in Savaii. Everything is slower here. More purposeful. Uncluttered by the traffic, bustling commerce and crowds of Upolu. Our vans stop for pigs to cross the road with lazy swishes of their tails. We cross fords through gently flowing rivers where children frolic and their mothers sit cross-legged on glistening rocks in the shallows, doing laundry. Soap bubbles float downstream in the rainbow sunshine.

But my good mood fades when we reach Mother's village. Throughout the official welcome, all my relatives take it upon themselves to tell me how fat I am. So what else is new? But it seems a bit much to be expected to take it from people who haven't seen you since you were seven years old? Like, really Auntie-Old-Wrinkly-Bag-Of-Bones? You haven't seen me since I was wetting the bed and picking my nose in church? Of course I'm bigger now. It's been twenty-three years and I even got taller and grew boobs.

But I say nothing. I smile. Listen. Nod. Smile some more.

Everyone knows I am the cousin who has come from America, so there's lots of comments about McDonalds and KFC. About what a lazy life we lead over there, swimming in bathtubs of easy money and eating ourselves sick every day on cartons of Spam. For some reason, my aiga think that rich people eat Spam and McDonalds every day.

Still I say nothing. I listen. Smile. Listen some more. But in my head, I'm biting back...

'No actually, I'm working two jobs in the States so I can afford to send money home every week to help support my parents. Cousin Fili, didn't I send $500 for your mother's funeral last year? And Aunty Tala, that money my mother gave for building your new church? I sent that. You think that dropped out of the sky? I didn't get that by stuffing my face at McDonalds. I got it from working my ass off so you can relax here in the fale talimalo, weaving mats that you never finish because 'weaving' is actually code for gossiping about everybody.'

But no. I swallow the bitterness and judgement, and smile. My patience is sorely tested by Uncle Savelio though. He's a cousin of Mother's and once lived in America before being deported. It was a long time ago but you'd think he was there yesterday the way he starts going on and on about 'those Mexicans stealing all the jobs and isn't it a good thing they're going to build a wall now Scarlet?' *Oh fuck, my uncle is a Trump supporter.* Not what I expected to stumble across in Savaii. I mutter something unintelligible and try to scuttle away but he's excited to have another America-dweller to talk to. Or rather to give him nods of support as he rattles on about the good old days before Obama the anti-Christ.

Somebody save me.

Naomi presents her new husband to Great-Aunty, along

with a generous haul of wedding gifts that we have trucked along with us. I can't see much of the action though because I'm stuck listening to Uncle Savelio. I finally fake a headache and escape. Mother glares at me for running away but I pretend I don't see her. *Hey, I'm not the one who just got married so I don't need to suffer through all the ceremonial welcoming and blah blah'ing.*

Beyonce finds me and together we go to the nearby freshwater pool with some cousins. The water is sparkling clear and the refreshing coolness is glorious. It's the pool looked after by the Village Women's Komiti and only for the women so we can swim in just a lavalava and luxuriate in the privacy.

"Aaah this is the life," says Beyonce as she floats on her back. "Let's never go back to Apia!"

"Let's never go back to the family gathering from hell either," I laugh. "Just leave Naomi and Troy to face the wolves on their own."

"Yes, we're not missing anything important," agrees Beyonce.

We swim until the sun sets and then make our way back to the house where we are dutiful daughters and help with the dinner preparations.

Later that evening though, it seems we did miss something of vital importance. We are playing cards inside our mosquito net when Uncle Savelio's voice thunders in

Samoan over a portable loudspeaker, loud enough for the whole village to hear.

"Get up everyone. Come here. We must have a serious meeting, eh! Everyone. All the kids, all the adults, everyone."

Everyone shuffles into the faletalimalo, some murmuring in complaint, some excitedly faikala'ring – until they catch sight of Uncle's glare and quickly shush into false downcast obedience.

He doesn't keep us in suspense for long, launching into a masterful tirade. It seems that our visit has coincided with an ongoing conflict between our aiga and another family in the next village. The origins are unclear. From what I can gather, it had something to do with roaming pigs and someone's boundary for their taro plantation. And earlier tonight, someone – or several someone's – from our aiga had stoned the other family's cookhouse roof.

"Who was throwing stones at Mikakolio's house ah?" Uncle demands. "Who was there? Who did it?"

He strides up and down the front of the fale, stopping every so often to point into the crowd, air-stabbing his finger with vehement emphasis. "Don't lie. Don't keep silent! God sees everything. He sees YOU! Somebody was throwing stones at Mikakolio's house and I know all those somebody's are right here in this fale. Stand up now. Confess. Who was throwing stones at the house?"

He is a righteous leader in this moment and I am

stabbed with guilt about how I had written him off as a nuisance Trump-loving windbag. *Good work Uncle Savelio. I don't know everything about this family feud with Mikakolio's aiga but you will put a stop to the foolishness before it escalates.* I smile at Uncle and send him vibes of support. He's just what this family needs. A strong leader with a sensible head on his shoulders.

But will the culprit own up? The taut silence stretches tighter and then snaps – as a little girl in a fluffy pink dress stands. She can't be more than eight years old.

"O a'u," she whispers as she stares at her dusty bare feet. "Me."

WTF?

Beside me, Beyonce chokes on a smothered laugh. Uncle glares at her impudence and then roars at all of us. "Who else?"

And then the floodgates open. A teenage boy stands, tying and retying his lavalava in nervousness. An elderly woman struggles to her feet, assisted by her daughter. Followed by a cluster of men at the far side of the fale. One by one, two by two until it seems half the entire crowd are standing, heads downcast.

My mind is blown. *Aunty Mina? Cousin Evelina? You too?* This is unreal.

Yes it seems the majority of my extended family were

stoning Mikakolio's house. I almost feel left out. Like everybody got invited to the party of the year and didn't ask me. Beyonce is laughing openly now, not even bothering to hide her mirth from Uncle's glare. Another dig in my side. "Oh they're gonna get it now!"

And then we wait with bated breath to see what Uncle will do next. For the sword of justice to fall.

Uncle Savelio surveys the guilty crowd with satisfaction. "Lelei. Good you confess."

Then he says, "I want to tell each and every one of you, how proud I am of you!"

Now Beyonce and I are really *What-The-Fuck*-ing? *Excuse me?*

Uncle Savelio continues. "You stood up for the name and the pride of our aiga. You are defending our honour." He beams, casting his approval far and wide. (But not to those of us who are non-stone-throwers of course. Because we did nothing to defend the family's honour. Useless family members who clearly have no loyalty or pride.)

"When anyone tries to offend someone in our family, then yes, you must show them the wrongness of their ways. You must stand up for us all."

The crowd of vigilantes are now holding their heads high, nudging each other, hi-fiving their own awesomeness.

Uncle Savelio isn't finished. "BUT!" he thunders. And everyone shushes again.

"There is a problem. When you go to get revenge on those people who be cheeky to us. You don't go in the open like that. No! That's how you end up in the jail. Sitting in Tafaigata, crying for your aiga to bring you some food. That's not how you do it. Don't stone their roof where everybody can see you and hear you."

Then his voice drops an octave and he hunches over, miming a sort of exaggerated Pink Panther-creep stance. "You must go quietly. In the dark. And KILL them. Strike like a ninja. You must creep up to them and stone them SECRETLY."

The last word is a shout into the mike and resonates into the shadows, startling chickens roosting in the breadfruit tree next to the fale. Where assorted villagers are sitting... faikala'ring, listening to every word being shouted in this Top Secret Family Meeting of assassins.

"Don't stone them loudly. Don't attack them publicly. That's stupid. I'm telling you the way to do it. Attack them secretly. And then the police won't catch you. And you won't go to Tafaigata."

This can't be real. I must be in a messed up messy Samoan novel about a fat woman who goes to Savaii for a family reunion and finds herself surrounded by an army of stealth warriors.

Beyonce mutters beside me, "Oh Lord it's a good thing your sister already got Troy to put a ring on it. Because if he'd seen just how crazy our family is, he would have run a mile in the opposite direction."

We both sneak a glance over at the newlyweds. They're oblivious and have eyes only for each other. Beyonce was right. True love makes us blind to all levels of crazy. Maybe not blind, but rather, it makes you focus on what really matters. Not the crazy. Not your family dramas. Just the person you love.

In that moment I'm so thankful that Jackson didn't come on this Savaii trip. Because my Savaii family of assassins would for sure have had him running miles away.

The next day I am summoned to the main fale for a weaving session with the women of the aiga. Presided over by Great-Aunty Pativaine who sits at the front of the fale in a wooden slat chair that's covered in colourful rag mats. Beside her several aunties take it in turns to fan her while she dozes.

I know everyone wants to see the plastic Samoan fail at weaving so I make sure to weave my section of mat with extra grace and precision. *Thank you Aunty Filomena for teaching us so well!* There's no breeze and sweat soaks my shirt as I weave industriously. But it's difficult to zone out the chatter around me, especially when so much of it is about us the visitors. Mother fields questions about her husband, her household back in Apia, her charity work, and all the wedding drama of the preceding month. Then it's Naomi's turn to be interrogated. Teased about her meauli husband. (*Tama uli dammit. Not meauli!*) Asked about their upcoming trip to America where Naomi will meet all Troy's aiga. And why is Naomi not resigning from her job at the Attorney General's office?

"You have a rich husband now," says one young cousin eagerly. "You don't have to work any more."

"Don't be stupid," remonstrates an older aunty. "Of course she should keep working."

Yay feminist aunty! I mentally cheer.

"Her husband isn't rich. It's his parents money and you know American parents don't look after their children like Samoans do. He's just a Pisikoa. That's not a real job. They got no money," contends the random Aunty. "Naomi has to wait until her husband gets a proper job."

Everyone says *Ahhhh* and nods in agreement, murmuring to each other about the shortcomings of families in America. I am glad this is a woman-only gathering and Troy is off with the cousins somewhere. Probably being subjected to the male version of this ordeal.

Then it's my turn to be the subject of the weaving conversation. They ask me about my life in America. How are my aunties there? That question is asked only to be polite because this is Mother's family and they don't like Father's family. (It's okay because the Aunties in America don't like Mother's family so it all balances out.) They ask about my work and I find myself telling them that while I work in a bakery, I also have been writing. Although I deliberately keep it vague what exactly I've been writing.

I sense rather than see Mother's surprise from across the fale. But I ignore it. I'm not sure why I'm telling my Savaii aiga that I'm a writer but it just seems right. Like it's time.

"You are a writer like your Father," says a random old Aunty. "Do you get money from it?"

I say yes. Everyone nods in acknowledgement of my success. Because there's no point writing books if you don't get money for it. Not like those people (*my Father*) who write books about the Bible because they're fiapoto and think the rest of us need the Bible explained to us. "Good girl," says random Aunty whose name I don't know. "You make our aiga proud."

My buzz at getting some praise is almost immediately killed though as another nameless Aunty asks, "What about a husband?"

I shake my head. "No husband. Just me."

A younger woman who I remember from my childhood – Dora I think? – speaks up. "Kalofae Scarlet, still no husband? It's because you're so fat. Kipi le ai. Stop eating so much. How is a man supposed to find your mea when you're so lapo'a?!" Yes she really did just ask, how is a man supposed to find my pussy when I'm so fat. *Thank you cousin Dora, bitch from hell.*

She has a nasal trilling voice, the kind that carries on the salt breeze and sends millipedes wriggling into the bushes in a frenzied rush to spread the news. She laughs and it seems like everyone in the fale laughs with her. Except for me and Beyonce. And Mother (because she doesn't laugh at crude, sexual humour. She has a religious reputation to uphold.)

Dora's taunt is no more hurtful than many others that have been thrown my way during this trip and before. We Samoans know how to wound with words, like no other. We are a culture of orators after all. I should shrug it off, like I have shrugged off words before. But for some reason, I don't. I can't. Not today.

I ignore Beyonce's fingernails that are digging into the tender flesh of my arm, take a deep breath and pitch my voice so it resonates. Loud. I want the flying foxes snoozing in the mango tree to hear it.

"Yes I'm fat. But at least men don't find their way to my mea because of how bad it smells. When's the last time you washed that stinky thing of yours? I should bring you some industrial soap from America next time I come."

Dora is so shocked that her mouth opens and shut several times. Like a fish. The whole house has gone quiet. A stunned kind of oppressive quiet like waiting for a cyclone. Everyone is staring with their faikala wires on high alert. We Samoans have highly refined memorisation skills, honed through many years of White Sunday tauloto practises. We don't need to push the audio record button on our phones. Every word and muffled *AWOLLA!* is being brain recorded and stored, ready to be replayed several times over for a future audience.

I'm not done. I figure, hey I'm dead already so may as well go out with a bang and give my relatives something to talk about during many Bingo nights to come.

I raise my voice another notch. "E lelei a'u ouke lapo'a e mafia ga lusi ae o oe ga e fagau mai auleaga e ke oki a o e auleaga. A least I can lose weight but you, you were born ugly and you'll die ugly. What's wrong with being fat? If I wanted to eat leaves and get skinny, I can. But you? With your ugly face and ugly heart? You're stuck with those forever."

My attack complete, the audience swings their hungry gaze to Dora. The ball is in her court now. *What you going to do Dora?* The woman splutters and fans herself with furious intensity, like she needs to cool down her shock and rage before she combusts. I suddenly remember that this is not my home ground. I have effectively waltzed into this woman's enclave and insulted her. She could jump up and beat my ass (with the willing assistance of any number of loyal friends) and she would be entirely justified in her violence. I can count on Beyonce to fight for me, but even her ferocity wouldn't be enough. We're outnumbered. The crowd would probably cheer and take bets on how much hair I will have left on my head by the time Dora's done.

My anger flees as quickly as it comes. *Uh oh.* Is it too late to apologise? Make a run for it? I could lock myself in the truck?

But before anyone can launch their campaign of vengeance, a wheezy cackly laugh breaks the strained quiet. Everyone turns. It's Great-Aunty Pativaine. I have never seen the old bat smile and here she is laughing so hard that tears stream down her face.

She points at me with a trembling hand. In Samoan she says, "You have courage. And what a mouth." She does an imitation of me. "*When's the last time you washed that stinky thing of yours?*" Another wheezy laugh. "Come sit here," she orders.

When Aunty Pativaine commands, you obey. I suppress the instinctive urge to run (and get on a plane and never come back), and walk over to where she sits. Another aunty I don't know is sitting in the chair beside her and Pativaine tells the woman impatiently, to go sit somewhere else. The woman gives me her seat, and the fan so I can take over fanning her Majesty.

I sit where I'm told. And wait. And fan. What does this ferocious creature want of me?

Across the fale I catch sight of Mother. She looks worried.

Auntie Pativaine takes a loud slurp of her tea and swishes it around her mouth before leaning forward to me.

"E sa'o lou kala." You speak true.

She throws Dora a look so scathing that I'm surprised she isn't riddled with holes or burnt to a crisp already. Then she says, "Her grandmother was a daughter of pigs. Never liked her. What can you expect when you come from such a line? Stupid girl."

Aunty doesn't bother to whisper. Why would you? When you're a hundred years old, you can say and do whatever you want. It almost makes me want to live that long so I can wield that kind of #NoFucksGiven superiority.

Aunty launches into a tale about Dora's long-dead grandmother (may she rest in peace). Something about how she married into the family, was perpetually lazy, never did any feau's, her weaving was shit, and she was always cheating at Bingo.

According to Aunty, she had been the worst kind of nofotane. The kind who didn't know her place and ate from the sapasui pot before important guests were served. Oh – and she had tried and failed to disagree with Great Aunty at a Women's Komiti meeting, so Aunty had thrown a pot of hot tea at her.

"Amio puaa," says Aunty Pativaine.

Okay then.

In my world, being the thrower of hot teapots makes you more of the amio puaa, rather than the person who was the target of said hot teapot? But then again, what world do I live in? One where the ancient are trundled off to rest-homes to rot. Not a world where they hold regal court and everyone quakes at the brittle snap of their voice and leaps to their command.

Another elderly woman tries to murmur soothing words of a peacemaker. Something about forgiveness and the perfect love of Jesus. But that only further infuriates Great Aunty. She hacks an awful raggedy sound and spits, aiming for outside the fale but instead only making it on the cement floor.

"Don't talk to me about forgiveness! My grandmother lived to be older than I am now, and she didn't know this Jesus. She was a fighter. For our aiga. For our land. None of this palagi peacefulness. That's why all of you are too soft. You forget Jesus wasn't Samoan. The palagi brought him here and now you recite his words like they are ours. Words that make our women weak."

I'm in stunned awe but there's a weary air of resignation in the fale. It's clear that for everyone else, this is not a new tirade.

Aunty continues, her voice gaining momentum. How is it possible that this wizened little old lady has this much power in her?

"Like YOU girl!" She points at Dora. "Every week your shit-eater husband beats you, and every Sunday the faifeau tells you to forgive. Every time you cry to these women and what do they tell you? They tell you onosa'i, be patient. Loto maualalo, be humble. They read you the Bible to be a good wife because Jesus said so. Then every week he beats you again and everyone hears it and does nothing."

"But you know what my mother did when my father tried to beat her? She waited until he was asleep and she cut off his poki. Then her mother and her sisters chased him out of the village. He never dared to show his face around here again. Everybody told the story everywhere as a reminder of what happens when you disrespect a woman of our family. Ha. He was no use to any woman after that. No poki!"

Aunty cackles uproariously and I am sorely tempted to laugh too. But then I catch sight of Mother's scandalised glare. Good girls don't use the word poki. And they certainly don't laugh at the thought of a woman cutting a man's penis off.

"Your mother should pray less and do more to fight for you Dora. But what do you expect? Daughter of pigs. All of you. If I had a sapelu I could do it." Aunty mimes a vicious cutting motion and there is grim glee on her face. "If you were true warriors and bring him to me, I could do it!"

Nobody raises an eyebrow and again I see that Great-Aunty's threats of violence are nothing new. They probably keep all the knives within a 100m radius locked up securely.

Then Dora lets out a loud aggrieved wail of protest, as she tries to say something in outraged defence of her maternal ancestry. Or perhaps in defence of her husband's privates?

Immediately two women next to her – leap up and slap her face. One slap. Two. Then a fuki of her hair just for good measure. *How dare you contradict the Matriarch!?* An older version of Dora, her mother? – comes running from outside the fale and tugs at Dora's hair bun, dragging her up and out of the assembly. Muttering and berating her as she goes.

Now mother's look of concern makes sense. She's freaking out that I might shame us all by saying something stupid in front of Great Aunty. I'm sure Mother's hands are itching to give me a pre-emptive slap and yank me out of here by my hair before I can open my mouth again.

Great Aunty's lip curls as she watches the offender get removed. She has a large mole on the right side of her upper lip and I'm finding it hard not to stare as it wobbles every time she purses her mouth.

She looks back at me and the intensity of her stare has me sitting up straight – but then slouching back down again as I remember that here, one doesn't show respect by standing tall. Especially not taller than the tiny elder beside you. *So confusing sometimes to be straddling two cultures. Dammit.*

Aunty doesn't care about my inner cultural turmoil. "You're the girl they sent away to live in America."

I nod and then remember my manners. "Yes Aunty."

There's a sly gleam in her eyes. "You're the girl who was drunk and pua'i at the funeral."

The coconut wire is strong, reaching all the way here. I cannot turn away from the shark noose rope trap of her gaze that tells me she knows. *You're the girl who got pregnant and had an abortion? You're the girl who did bad things?*

I nod again and steel myself for what comes next.

"I never liked him," Aunty says with a sneer.

Excuse me?

"He was not a good boy. Even when he lived here with your grandparents. He was maka'i fale."

All the noise of just-another-day in Savaii dims and fades. There is no one here but me, Great-Aunty. And Mother, who is sitting still and with a face like stone.

"I told my sister he was a bad one. She tried to beat it out of him with lots of Jesus, but he had a sickness inside. How did he die?" asks Aunty.

I pretend ignorance. "Who?"

She gives me a look of disgust. "Solomona. Who else."

"Cancer," I say disguising my inner screaming with abject politeness.

Aunty shakes her head. "No. It was ma'i Samoa. Spirit sickness. A curse." She says it with such obvious relish that for a moment I am afraid of her, thinking of dark whisperings about aitu and teine Sa. "The aitu sends the rotting sickness to such men. Was it in his poki?"

Great-aunty seems slightly obsessed with penises.

"No, not his prostate. I think it was lung cancer."

Aunty isn't dissuaded. A sage nod. "Telesa matagi sends ma'i Samoa in the air. You can't hide from them." She gives me a laser sharp glare. "It was different when we were the feagaiga. When the word of a daughter, a sister carried the power. Any man who did the things he did? No matter how old or young. No matter who he was. Would have been shamed. Punished. Driven out of the nu'u. In the old times, your mother would have cut him." She mimes a vigorous slashing motion, the glee evident on her face.

Okay then.

I purposely avoid looking at Mother on the other side of the fale. I don't want to see the anger in her eyes. The condemnation. I have weathered enough of it to last me several lifetimes. I didn't bring up Solomon. This is all Great-Aunty.

There's a long pause and it seems like Aunty has fallen asleep, her head dropping in a dozy slumber. I am about to get up and creep away, make my escape while Dora is getting chastened by her mother. There's still time for me to make it to the truck.

But then Pativaine's head jerks up and her eyes glare right at me.

"Do you see..." she pauses with a furrowing of her wrinkly brow, then turns to snap at the nearest daughter in attending. "O lea le igoa o le kama o le aka foi gale?" What's the name of that actor again?

They don't know the answer and so they look fearful.

Aunty is impatient and spits curse words at them. They are shit eaters, dumber than the actual ass of an ass, and their grandmothers are peeing in their graves at how ashamed they are of such ignorant descendants.

Finally, one of the lesser aunts hazards a cautious guess. And yes she's correct!

Aunty Pativaine is gleeful. "Rambo!" she says. "Sylvester Stallone. Do you see him there in America? He's my favorite. Very manaia."

Great Aunty is a Rambo fan? I wasn't expecting that.

"Well, he did come to Vegas last winter I think. I saw him." On the TV. Along with fifty million other people.

Aunty is delighted. "You saw him? What did you think? What's he like? Did he look the same as in the movies?"

I don't want to tell her that I haven't seen any of Stallone's movies. "Ummm, yes he does. Exactly the same. Very handsome. Big muscles. And a very nice man." Like me and Rambo are besties. And I was standing only a breath away from his muscles.

"What's your favorite Rambo movie?" she demands.

I hazard the safest guess possible. "The first one."

It's the right answer because she nods with grim seriousness. "The second one was alright but not as good."

She then launches into a monologue about Stallone's performance in lots of different movies. I say monologue because it's clear that she doesn't expect me to say anything. My contribution to this conversation is to listen in wide-eyed appreciation and nod every so often. I'm just glad she's not lacerating me with a recital of all my ancestor's sins. Out of the corner of my eye I see Mother relaxing visibly. *Have a little faith in me mom! I got this.*

It seems all one needs to do to be in Great Aunty's good books, is to say you saw Rambo in real life and lie about loving his movies, because when it's time for us to leave to catch the last boat back to Upolu, she pulls me tight in a wiry-armed hug.

After planting a wet kiss on my cheek she looks me in the eye and says with matter of fact casualness, "I will die soon. You won't see me again. So listen from in here." She stabs at my chest with a bony finger.

"You are too much living afraid. Solomona is dead. The aitu of our family is still watching over us women. Even though we try to forget them with Jesus. Don't waste their justice and suffocate in fear of a dead man." A nod at the other women in the fale where somewhere there is Dora. "That fire you showed? Speak it more. Live it more. Then you can be like me."

I try to think of something to say but Aunty is done, waving me away with sour impatience as she yells for someone to bring her tobacco leaves. I'm walking to the car when Aunty calls out with a loud voice. "Remember, always keep a sapelu by your bed! And don't be afraid to use it when you take a man in there." She makes that vicious slashing motion again that's scary even though her arms are skin and bone.

Relationship advice for every woman – keep a machete by your bed and make sure your man knows you can use it.

In the car to the wharf, Mother complains loudly about Great Aunt's blasphemy. She is thankful that Father was not there to hear it. (In that is an unspoken warning not to repeat a word of the incident to anyone in case it reaches Father's ears of judgement.) She mourns the passing of her mother, because "Only she could talk sense to Aunty." She tells us never to follow Pativaine's example of disrespect and sacrilege. "Everyone is so scared of her. Oka! And she wonders why I never want to go visit her."

I say something about Aunty being old and hasn't she earned the right to be as outspoken as she wants to be?

Mother makes a snort of disgust. "She was always like that. Even when I was a small girl. Always speaking things she shouldn't."

I think about Great-Aunty all the long ferry ride and drive home. I'm not surprised or even troubled that she knows about Solomon. This is Samoa where everyone knows everything about everyone. But it's her admonition that keeps echoing... *You are too much living afraid.*

Is she right? And if so, what am I afraid of?

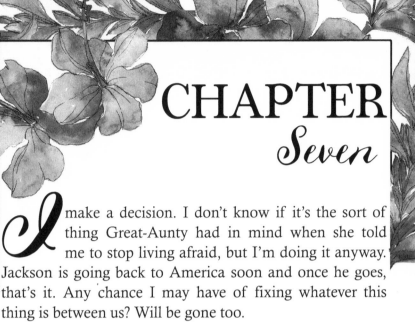

CHAPTER
Seven

I make a decision. I don't know if it's the sort of thing Great-Aunty had in mind when she told me to stop living afraid, but I'm doing it anyway. Jackson is going back to America soon and once he goes, that's it. Any chance I may have of fixing whatever this thing is between us? Will be gone too.

I go to the hotel, ask at the front desk for directions to Jackson's room and the woman at reception gives me a look of disdain.

"Mr. Emory? Is he expecting you?" she asks. The way she says his name, in a caressing kind of way tells me that she knows who Jackson is. She's noticed him.

Every jealous particle of me bristles, like it would if I were Jackson's girlfriend and had a right to be jealous and bristly. I want to say, *Bitch please, he has licked me from head to toe like a starving man with an ice cream sundae who just can't get enough.*

But I don't. I am here to grovel and apologise to Jackson and I'm not sure how my grovelling will be received. He could very well call for security to escort me from the building and then this evil snake will laugh at me.

So instead I smile with barbed sweetness. "Yes he most certainly is. Waiting. For me to come." I may have placed undue breathy emphasis on *cooooome*.

Without batting an eye, the receptionist hits back. "You should know the hotel has a policy about women visiting men's rooms."

Only in Samoa. Now I want to smack her.

"Really? I wonder how Mr Emory will feel when he finds out that I can't make our very important meeting because a ....receptionist tried to bar me from the room." I put on my most efficient corporate-sounding voice. The one where I sound like a palagi who went to Cambridge University and then had tea with the Queen. The voice every brown person knows will get us better service and more respect. Yes, we even use that voice on each other. Because it works. "I may have to file a complaint with your manager. This is unacceptable behaviour and not the standard of service I would expect from what's supposed to be Samoa's best hotel." I'm going to add in more, like – *'I wonder what the local newspaper would make of this story!'* and *'You can be certain I will be writing a detailed unfavourable review on Trip Advisor! And taking this matter to social media in the worst way possible!'* But I don't need to. The woman backs off immediately. I stride away with my head held high and my back ironing-board straight, hoping that I radiate #bossBitch vibes. But as soon as I get to Jackson's door, my fake white people confidence fades.

What am I doing here? Am I really doing this?

Deep breath. I knock and from within I hear his muffled voice. "Coming." Footsteps. "You can just put it here."

The door opens and the words trail away when he sees me. "You're not room service."

My rehearsed speech disintegrates at the sight of him. "You're not wearing any clothes," I say.

Because he isn't. Jackson Emory is standing in the doorway with nothing but a towel tied at his hips. It's a small towel and Jackson Emory is a very big man. He's just stepped out of the shower and droplets of water glisten on every line and muscled curve of his torso. He was shaving because he's got a razor in one hand and half his face still has a froth of white cream on it.

He's a tall drink of ice vai tipolo on a steaming hot day. Brown sugar gritty on your tongue, crunchy sweetness in your mouth.

There's surprise on his face and then quickly replaced with a mask of reserve. "Scarlet. I wasn't expecting you."

And I wasn't expecting you to be naked, but hey, life's full of unexpected blessings.

"Can I come in?" I ask. Please say yes. Please.

He opens the door wider and steps back. "Of course."

Even in my current state I can still appreciate the

splendour of the finest suite money can buy in Samoa.

"Wow. This is fancy." I suddenly feel very dirty and very poor. I showered before I came over but maybe I should have gone to the salon and gotten my hair done too. Booked a makeup artist. *This was a bad idea. I need to go.* I clamp down on my inner panic. Because the blood of poki-chopping warrior women runs in my veins and I can do this.

"Please, sit down, make yourself comfortable." He points to his face. "Let me finish up. I'll be quick."

"Sure. I'll wait."

He disappears through another door, but doesn't close it so he can call out over the sound of a tap running. "I thought you were Afa with the breakfast order. He's great. Gives me a commentary every morning on his night out…" Then there's a sharp exclamation.

"Did you cut yourself?" I call out.

He reappears in the doorway, frowning, one hand to his jaw. "How did you guess?"

"I say *fuck* too when I cut myself shaving my legs."

There's blood leaking through his fingers now and he looks around to grab tissue to staunch it.

I take refuge in being efficient and medically proficient. I've watched every season of Grey's Anatomy. I got this.

"Sit down, let me help."

He obeys and I go to study the cut. "Wow it's a big one. You're careless, aren't you."

A frown. "I was in a rush."

"Oh? Nervous because I walked in on you naked?" I tease.

"Half-naked," he corrects me. "I have a towel on."

I scoff. "That little thing? Oh Jackson please, it barely covers anything."

Our eyes and smiles meet and it's a perfect moment of lightness, one worth savouring. One I put in my pocket of memories, storing for later when I go back to my real life.

I help him clean up and stick a bit of plaster on his jawline before he goes to put some clothes on, re-emerging in a white shirt and pants. *How is it possible that I want to have sex with him even more when he has clothes on?*

"I thought you'd left already," I said. "But Troy said your flight got cancelled."

He nodded. "Yeah. Something about donkeys on the runway? Getting sucked into the plane engine?"

I make a yuck face. "Ugh, only in Samoa!"

"Can I get you something to drink?" he asks. Without waiting for a reply he goes to the bar on the opposite side of the room. Ice and Diet Coke.

"Oh, no champagne?" I quip because I'm nervous and I always say dumb things when I'm nervous.

The careful way that he hands me the glass tells me he's feeling some of the caution and anxiety that I've got bubbling inside me.

That glimpse gives me reassurance. I take a deep breath as we both sit on opposite sides of the couch.

"I came to talk to you about what happened at the hospital..." I say, ready to do this right. But he interrupts.

"No, let me say something first, please," he says. "I was out of line. I have no business telling you how to be with your family. I shouldn't have said what I did and I'm sorry." He runs a hand through his hair as he frowns. "We only just met and I got no right to step in like that. I hate seeing you unhappy, or anyone – even your family – disrespect you like that. But the more I learn about Samoan culture and how families work here, the more I realise how out of line I was. This is new, we're new and I overstepped. I hope I haven't screwed everything up."

I look at this man who radiates earnest apology and all I can think is how bad I want to hold him, hug him, kiss him and love him. I move to his side of the couch and lay a finger against his lips.

"Shhh Jackson. Stop talking. I'm sorry too."

And then I kiss him. For a heartbeat he is frozen with surprise, and then he is kissing me back. It's languorous and slow, tongue play so delicious that I feel like I could do this all day, and all night. I want to weep at how right it feels. How kissing him feels like returning to a home I never knew I had. Safe, secure, familiar, forever welcome.

But then it gets hungry. His hands come up to tug me closer, the kiss deepens and I want – I need – to get closer.

I pause for a moment – so I can straddle him, so I can better hold his face in my hands, so I can drink him in. I can feel his hardness, a growing surging heat between my widespread legs and I grind against him instinctively. He groans, reaches up to fist a handful of my hair so he can pull my head back, so he can kiss the line of my throat, and then down to the wire of electricity that runs along my shoulders. A muttering that sounds a lot like a curse word when my shirt gets in the way.

"Off," he demands, curt and rough.

I like curt and rough Jackson!

I'm tugging at my shirt but it's too slow for him and before I can register what's happening – he grips the fabric with two hands and rips it open. A sound of triumph and then he is peeling down the lace cups of my bra. The sound of my breathing is loud in the suite but not as loud as my mewling cry when he suckles first one breast and then the other. His mouth is hot and wet and he sucks, licks and nibbles with a fierceness that both hurts and feels very, very good at the same time.

I am rubbing against him now in a regular bucking rhythm and the barrier of our clothing has me whimpering with frustration. I want to move off his lap so I can unzip him, so I can get the last of our clothes out of the way, but he won't let me. Instead he grips both breasts in his big hands and centres me.

Another command. "Be still."

This is a Jackson I haven't seen before. Authoritative and in control. *I love it.*

He holds me still on his lap so he can tease each turgid nipple with his tongue, lapping at them and making me squirm as he gently pinches and tweaks the thick buds.

"So does this mean you accept my apology," I gasp, trying to joke and lighten the moment but failing miserably because he's doing things that make any conversation impossible. So I just rock against him instead and give myself over to the waves of delight.

"See how beautiful you are Scarlet?" he says, voice thick with desire as he looks up at me. "I can't get enough of you."

Seeing the stark need in his eyes is an incredible thrill. *Jackson wants me. Needs me.*

But then the hunger in his eyes is replaced with something else. Something deeper and more intense. He stops what he's doing.

"Before we do this. Before we go any further. I want to be clear."

I'm trying not to curse with frustration. *Stop now? Can't we talk later?* "Yes, anything you want. Anything you say. Let's talk about it later. After." I try to kiss him again. But he stops me.

"No. I can't do this until we get this straight." He leans back into the sofa and looks up at me. "This. You. Me. Us. This isn't a holiday thing. Or a casual thing. Or whatever other words you used to describe it. I want more Scarlet. This doesn't end here in Samoa. I have to go home but I want to see you again."

"You do?" I ask stupidly. Really? Why?

Jackson smiles. It's all for me and it's beautiful. "Yes. And I'm not going to keep pretending in front of your family that we aren't lovers. I know we have to be careful here and follow certain protocols according to Samoan culture, but I'm going to tell everyone that we're dating."

"We are?" I say, even more stupidly than before.

His face darkens and there's a hint of questioning in his eyes. "Unless I have it all wrong and you don't want us to take this further? Because there's nothing I want more right now than to take you into that bedroom and make love to you, but I can't do casual with you. I don't want to do casual with you."

"You don't?" I am a broken record with this man and his declarations right now. "No casual?"

"No casual." Again the grin and the Jason Momoa eyebrow action has my insides – and outsides- incinerating with so much I WANT YOU fire. "I want your family to know about us. Your friends. Your aunties back in Vegas. Everyone who's important to you. I'd like to meet them."

Oh shit.

"I'm not sure that's a good idea," I say. "Let's agree we're dating but we can keep it between us." Problem solved, right? I move against him, just a little, hoping to get him back to the truly important things in life. Like us getting our freak on. *Now. Now. Now.* I want him to touch me so bad that I am faint with the longing. I have never contemplated tying anyone up but I might be tempted if this man doesn't hurry up and take us to third base.

Again he stops me. This time wrapping his arms around me so I am encircled in his embrace, velvet bands of steel. The coconut rough grate of his voice whispering against my ear, sends tugging's of wired heat through me.

"Scarlet, you will tell your family about us. You will give us a real chance."

My frizz of wild hair has burst free of it's bun, exuberantly joining the party that is Scar's rainforest of sin. I pull away and peek out at him from behind a tangle of hair. "And if I say no?"

He is trying to gauge how serious I am. Then his eyes narrow. "Then we don't do this." He releases me and folds his arms in front his chest. There is a lazy drawl to his voice as he says, "Are you ashamed of me?"

"Of course not! I adore every delicious divine inch of you." I pounce, capturing his mouth with mine. An eager searching kiss. He responds with a fierceness that equals my own and I am triumphant. *Yes! I win. Enough with this needless talking-talking-talking!* I move against him, grinding because I just can't help it.

He groans. Jackson actually groans. A rough ragged sound that tells me he wants this as much as I do. That's when he says, "We aren't doing this here."

We aren't?

He tucks his arms around me and stands, lifting me like I'm cotton candy and not the sack of taro that I am. I yelp as I instinctively wrap my legs around him and hang on tight. "Put me down! I'm too heavy. You're going to break your back."

He ignores me and doesn't pause as he carries me to the bedroom. The bed is huge. Crisp white sheets in the afternoon sunlight that streams in through the glass panelled doors. He lays me down and then pulls his shirt up and over his head. There it is, the broad expanse of contoured muscle and ridged abs, the obliques that play a starring role in my fantasies. I smile. Then a frown as I think of the bitchy receptionist. The awful image flashes across my mind, of her standing outside, giving me the grand middle finger of disapproval as she calls for Security to come escort my skanky ho ass out of their fancy hotel.

"What is it?" asks Jackson.

"The curtains. Can you shut them?"

A wolfish grin as he complies. "Okay, but you are not hiding anything from me." He pushes a button on the remote and dim lights chase away the dark shadows. "I want to see all of you while we're making love."

"I kinda don't want you to. Do you have to?"

"Yes." He advances towards the bed and I sit up on my elbows, watching him.

He unbuckles his belt and drops his shorts, kicking them to the side. He's not wearing any briefs and I'm staring at the size of him. There is no denying that he is very happy to see me.

There's a wild gleam in his eyes as he moves through the shadows towards the bed. I look up at him and it seems even the very air in the room is delicious with anticipation. I reach for him but he stills me with a taut command. "Lie back."

I obey. Because when a naked Jackson tells you to lie back, you do it. At this point I think I would lie on a bed of millipedes if he told me to.

He kneels, trails a delicate frolic of kisses along my thighs, casting a web of electric sinnet that has me caught, poised in anticipation but also reluctance. The other times had been urgent, risky, time-sensitive driven encounters and here now, everything is deliberate. Planned. Suddenly, I'm shy. He gently parts my legs that now, are unsure about giving him access. Because now there's time and space for him to really see how fat I am. My scars. My everything.

But then in the dim light, I hear him murmur, "So beautiful Scarlet. So perfect. I've been wanting so bad to taste you again."

He hooks his broad arms around my upright legs. The first lick of his tongue is scorching fire, burning away any shyness. The second banishes any remnant of unsureness. Then he settles into a rhythm, slow, sensual and decadent. Light hot licks of delight. Like we have all the time in the world and he never wants to stop.

I'm not worrying any more about bitchy receptionists reporting me to security. Or what my aunties will say if a faikala taxi driver tells them he saw me visiting a man's hotel room. My hands are on his head now, fingers threaded thru his hair, caressing him, urging him on.

I'm making awfully loud whimpering sounds now, but I don't care. Because there's liquid chocolate running in my veins and a building crescendo of joyful sound, rushing, pulsing and building – with each expert lick and thrust.

And then he stops. *What? Why?*

I half sit up and he looks up at me with a wicked grin. "This is on. We are dating. We tell your family."

For a moment I am confused, because good licking can have that effect on a person. "Wait, what? You're not serious?!"

He nods. Then moves to hold himself above me, with his legs on either side of me. "No more hiding. No more sneaking around. Repeat after me Scarlet."

He is doing delicious things with his mouth again. A trail of deliciousness from my neck to my breasts where he settles in with a murmur of appreciation.

"That's not fair Jackson," I gasp. "You're torturing me into saying yes!" I thread my fingers through his hair, clutching at silken handfuls, savouring the magic he wreaks everywhere.

Again he stops. This time to ask, "And is it working?"

This is nuts. He's nuts. Of course we can't tell my family that we're 'dating'. Samoans don't date for fuck's sake. And no amount of the most heavenly licking of the most sensitive parts of me is going to change that.

But then I'm not thinking any more because my whisper thin control snaps and I'm a blazing shuddering mess. And he's holding me in his arms, murmuring sweet delicious things in my ear as I shatter.

Some time later, it could be minutes, it could be an hour, I am looking up at him as he lies next to me propped up on one elbow.

"What was that?" I ask.

"Round one," he says with that wicked grin. "Are you ready for round two? I am. But!" He turns serious. "I want to hear you say it. We go public. And you will let me take you out when we're back stateside."

This beautiful man doesn't get it. No woman with half a brain, 'goes public' with a man in Samoa, unless they're a certain level of serious. Take Naomi for example. She narrowly escaped being tagged a paumuku with her assorted 'public dates' because she had actually gotten engaged to two of them. Before Troy. So what if that meant everyone talked behind her back about having two broken hearted fiances? Besides, she was married now so that wiped her sins clean. How could Jackson and I ever be anything more than this? This wild, amazing, great sex connection we had going on? I still wasn't sure why he was wasting his time on me, but I fully expected him to wake up to his foolishness the minute he landed back in the US. I was preparing myself for that but in the meantime, did I really want all my cousins and aunties and sisters and nephews and nieces to know about him? To bear eventual witness to my heartbreak and shame when Jackson ended it with me?

But then he slides deep inside and it feels so good, so right, so perfect that all my Very Good Reasons for keeping us secret, suddenly seem like fluff in the wind. He thrusts again and I groan, a ragged gasping sound in the whirling storm of delight, the Category Five called Jackson Emory. I am arching my back, urging him on, desperately trying to hold on to that cliffside edge he is rushing me towards – when he stops. Poised above me, a hand fisted in my thick tangle of hair. His eyes sear me with their intensity.

"Say it Scarlet. Say yes to me. To us."

And all the reasons why I should say no are swept away before the storm.

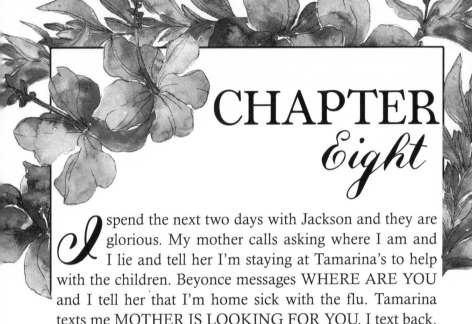

CHAPTER
Eight

I spend the next two days with Jackson and they are glorious. My mother calls asking where I am and I lie and tell her I'm staying at Tamarina's to help with the children. Beyonce messages WHERE ARE YOU and I tell her that I'm home sick with the flu. Tamarina texts me MOTHER IS LOOKING FOR YOU. I text back, IM WITH BEYONCE. DON'T WORRY.

Lies. And I don't even feel bad. I don't worry about my eternal damnation because I'm too busy savouring Jackson.

We make love. Again and again. And then again. We order room service. He feeds me cheesecake and slices of mango, and does things with whipped cream that were surely never included in any recipe books anywhere. Delicious, sweet, sticky and messy things. Then he carries me to the shower where he proceeds to remove all the evidence. Slowly. I used to read about shower sex and be doubtful, because how could it possibly work in such a slippery wet and steamy small space? Jackson shows me how wrong I was. *Oh so very wrong.* I also learn important things about in-the-Jacuzzi sex. On the sofa sex. And take-turns-to-tie-each-other-up sex.

We talk and laugh and talk some more, late into the night. I am famished because lots of good sex will do that to a person. Make you incredibly, happily hungry. We order more food. Over pizza he tells me about life growing up with his foster brothers, the parents who eventually adopted them all. He has me laughing uproariously with stories of how he met Troy at college and all their adventures since. He knows enough about my family so I tell him about Nina and our shared life in Vegas. My writing, how excited I was to sign with a literary agent and to now have two of my books optioned for film.

"They may not come to anything," I explain, "an option is no guarantee they will ever make a movie, but it's exciting anyway." I frown. "Part of me hopes they don't make a movie though, because then my parents will really find out what kind of books I'm writing. Ouch."

He doesn't dismiss my worries with platitudes about *'Oh just don't worry about them...you're a grown woman and don't need your parent's approval anymore...'*

No, he knows too much about me and our Samoan culture for him to give me advice like any random palagi would. Instead his eyes are soft as he reaches out to caress my cheek. A soft, lingering touch as he cradles my face in his hands. "You've come so far with your writing and you'll know when the time is right for your family to know more. I'm so in awe of you no matter what. A book deal and film options? My girlfriend is kickass amazing!"

I grin. I can't help it. "Girlfriend huh?" I fake a look

around. "Where?"

His answer is to gently push me back against the sheets so he can kneel above me, holding me captive. A hot kiss at the base of my throat. The rasp of his tongue along the skin of my neck and shoulder as he murmurs, "Right here. She's my prisoner."

"Oh really? What are you going to do with your prisoner?"

"Anything and everything that I want," he growls as he pins my arms above my head.

The promise sends a thrill of heat through me and I throw my head back and lose myself to the joy that is Jackson Emory. And when we are content, I fall asleep in his arms. Replete. Safe. Happy.

I never want to go home. But I have to eventually. Back to reality. I can't lie forever that I'm at Tamarina's and looking after the children, even though I want to!

It's 6am when I get home. Cousin Siaosi and his little brother are already half-done with making the saka, fanning the smoke away from their sweaty faces. Cousin gives me a knowing look.

"I hope it was worth it girl!" he whispers with a cheeky grin.

I can't stop the big smile in my face, so I give him the

finger before I go inside. The boys laugh quietly in the dawn.

So this is what 'walking on air' feels like. I'm floating as I unlatch the back door and tip toe inside the kitchen. I should go upstairs immediately and fake sleep before anyone else catches me, but I'm hit with a sudden stab of hunger so fierce that I almost stumble in my tracks. *If I don't eat NOW, I'm going to die dammit!*

I guess having four orgasms in one night will do that to a girl.

Praise Jesus for Aunty Filomena, there's a pot of chop-suey leftovers in the fridge and umu breadfruit in the sefe. The chop-suey is cold and the breadfruit is dry, but I don't care. I had wild sex all night and everything tastes like cake and ice-cream to me now.

I'm grinning to myself as I shovel chop-suey in my mouth, when Mother's voice from the doorway, has me freeze mid-swallow.

"Where have you been?"

I turn. "What do you mean?" I stall.

For a moment I am five years old all over again and dreading Mother's temper, the hot sting of the salu on my legs. I flashback over a lifetime of scriptures and #goodGirl preaching. Shame and guilt tattooed on my soul. I think of all the wickedly delicious things I just did with Jackson and I burn with shame and guilt.

Mother advances. "You've been gone for two days. But I looked for you at your sister's house and you weren't there. Where were you? Who with? Where is your respect? Where is your love for your aiga?" Her lip curls as she looks me up and down with disgust.

I should deny. Lie. Cry. Apologise. Then deny, lie, cry and apologise some more.

But I don't. I can't.

I raise my head up high and speak truth. "I was with my boyfriend." Okay, so I stumble over the word B O Y F R I E N D, but hey, I say it. Give me a medal for bravery.

Mother flinches. Then she launches herself at me, flailing, slapping and hitting. Screaming (but quietly so the neighbors don't hear), "Paumuku! Whore."

At first I let the blows rain on me. A lifetime of conditioning requires it. But then I break and grab her hands. "No. Stop it."

It's shock more than anything else that stops her. Shock that I have dared to answer back. I push her away and walk to the other side of the kitchen, putting the table between us.

"I won't let you hit me. Yes I'm your daughter, but I'm thirty years old and you don't get to make me small anymore."

The shock on her face almost makes me laugh. Almost.

"What's happened to you?" she demands. "I didn't teach you to be like this. Where is your respect? You have no gratitude. No alofa. No love for your family, your parents." The look of condemnation on her face would have made the old Scarlet, cringe and break into a thousand pieces. But not now. Not this time.

My voice is calm and sure. "Of course I love my family and I will always be grateful to you my parents for everything you have done for me. But I'm not a child anymore and I won't let you treat me like one."

Her lip curls in a sneer. "You will always be a child! A spoilt, foolish, ungrateful child. You bring nothing but shame to this family. Why can't you be like your sisters?"

Not that again. I stop myself from a weary eye-roll. "I love each of my sisters. We are all quite different. I wish you wouldn't try to compare and make us compete against each other all the time." I'm trying to hold fast to reason and calmness. No matter how psycho my mother gets, I will not be swept into her particular waterfall of crazy.

Well that's what I tell myself anyway, until she advances on me and comes around the table, determined. I know that look on her face. She may not be brandishing a salu, but she's got fasi on her mind.

"Stop this," I say firmly. "This is stupid. Why can't we sit down and talk, have a proper conversation, like adults?"

She gives me another look of disgust. She is shaking with rage. "Don't bring those palagi ways here. But then, you were always like that. A bad girl. I tried. We all tried, but you never listened. And it's us your family who pay the price for your selfish actions. Even from a young age you were a bad girl. Getting pregnant."

Now I'm losing it. "If we're going to talk about bad behaviour, let's talk about yours. What kind of mother are you anyway? I got pregnant because I was raped. What kind of mother punishes her child for something that wasn't her fault? How many times do I have to tell you? How was that my being a bad girl?"

This is new ground. Never have my mother and I spoken to each other like this. Never have we laid bare so many broken pieces of things long left buried. I hardly know myself. And my Mother also. I have only ever seen her this distraught once before. That afternoon many years ago when Father confronted us in his study.

Deep inside there is a whisper of warning. *Stop. Don't go any further. You are unleashing that which can never be taken back. You're not ready. Don't do this.*

But I hear Great-Aunty's voice once again. *You are too much living afraid.* And I know, that yes, I am ready. No more silence. No more secrets.

And so I do it. I launch my va'a into the ocean of no return. *Nafanua help us all.*

My mother snarls and in the early morning light, she's almost feral. "You're not a mother. You don't understand how it feels."

I call B.S. "You're wrong. The other night, I held Tamarina's baby in my arms and knew if anyone tried to hurt her, I'd do anything necessary to stop them," I say, fighting now, not to shout. Not to raise my voice to the heavens in righteous rage. "I'd give my life to keep her safe. I'm her aunty, not her mom and yet that's how I feel about her. That's how a mother should feel about her child."

She's shaking her head. There's a rigid line of obstinacy from wood floor panels to the furrowed broad forehead. Muttering. "A mother does what she must for her child. You'll never understand."

"How can you say that? After Solomon? Everything he did to me. You let him get away with it. Over and over again. I'm your daughter and you let him hurt me. Look at me mother, please." My voice breaks as I lay my soul on the ground at her feet. The woman I am now. The child that I was – and still am, deep within somewhere, still tightly holding on, still hoping, still fearing. I unwrap that final package of bitter bundled hurts and speak them out loud. Turmeric on my tongue.

"I'm your child. You didn't keep me safe." *Why? Mother please?*

She says nothing. I entrust her with my most fragile of fragments.

And she says nothing. Only stares at me, angry and defiant. Scornful.

In that silence, in that emptiness, all is revealed. The words I long for her to say. *I'm sorry. I didn't protect you. I'm sorry I didn't believe you.* She will never speak them. Say them. She will never be the mother I ache for her to be. She can't.

I confront my worst fear. And yet - I'm still breathing. The world is still turning. Outside, the chittering squeaks of the flying fox in the mango tree. Dogs bark at cars on the road. Chickens squawk as the neighbor's cat chases them around the yard. Life goes on. I have confirmed my worst fear about my mother and about myself, but I am okay. There is a surprising lightness of being that catches me by surprise. My mother didn't care for me the way she should have. She can't see why she was wrong, where she failed. She will never see it. And that's okay. Because one person's shittiness as a mother is not a reflection of the worth of her child.

She mutters again. More to herself than to me. "A mother does what she must for her child. You'll never understand."

Then it hits me. The worm snake of truth she does not speak. Even as it tries to squirm out of sight, underground, burrowing back into the comforting darkness of earth.

"Wait. Your child…you don't mean me, do you?"

There's a flicker of something elusive in her eyes.

Slippery glint of silver. A fish in the dark waters of the foul ocean that laps at the cement bracing of the fish market.

I can't breathe. It's too heavy. Too hot. Pressing down on me. The truth is too big for me to absorb. It's too much for me to bear. I'm trying but it's crushing me. Bones fragmenting to dust. "A mother does what she must for her child," I recite it tonelessly. A mantra that leads to enlightenment. "You're not talking about me."

"He was mine," she says. "I held him. Like this." In that moment she is not here. She is transported back in time, to a long ago past when she mothered a firstborn child that was not me. She cradles the specter of a long-dead baby in the crook of her arm and croons. "He was beautiful. Blue eyes and just a dusting of light brown hair. I wanted to call him Nigel. Like his father. But they took him. Gave him a good name from the Bible. Sent me away."

"It doesn't matter that I never raised him. Or I only got him back when he was grown. Or he believed Papa and Mama were his parents and I was his big sister. None of that mattered. Because I knew. Inside here." She beats at her chest. Fierce possession. I feel each fist batter against my own bruised heart. "He was always mine. My son. I always loved him. No matter what." She turns on me now and the air reeks of her resentment. "You're not a mother. You don't know anything about what it feels like. I do. I know. I protected my son."

"But what about me, your daughter? Solomon raped me."

"That wasn't rape." She shakes her head and the curl of her lip is laced with a kind of pity. "I know. You're my daughter and much like me. I know. I was fifteen when I had Solomon. His father was older. Married. Palagi here on a contract from Australia. I was weak. A bad girl. I brought shame to my family. But I was lucky. My parents didn't disown me. They had no sons so they decided to keep him as their own. I came to town to live with my aunty. I got a second chance. Everyone knew my sin but I got a second chance. Your father married me even knowing about my wrongs. He gave me a better life. He gave me penance and salvation."

I feel sick inside. "Father's not God." Hurt makes me cruel. "Is that why you've waited on him hand and foot all these years? Put up with his affairs?"

A step forward and she slaps me across the face. Hard. The sting of a hundred biting red ants.

"Shut your mouth. Whoever curseth his father, God curses." She chants scripture like it can save us all. Like it can make everything better. "Honor thy father and thy mother, that thy days may be long on the land that the Lord thy God giveth you."

"Everything you have, everything you are, is because of your father. He's a good man. Even after I never gave him a son. All the miscarriages. The failures. God's punishment on me for my childhood sin."

I protest. "You were a child. Fifteen. That man should

have known better. It was against the law for him to have sex with you."

She flinches at the mention of words that no decent Samoan parent should be hearing or saying in any decent conversations with their child. No matter how old they are. Obstinate distaste. "I sinned. And even after I tried my best to teach you God's ways, you were a sinner too. I failed you." For a brief moment she looks sad and there is apology in her. But too fleeting for me to grasp it. "But I knew my sin. Not you. You dared to blame Solomon for what happened. After you tempted him. He told me. We could all see it. You followed him everywhere. Bothered him all the time. Always laughed too loud. Talked too much. Wanting attention all the time. From your father. From me. From everyone. Always jealous of your sisters. Always. Tamarina the clever one. Envying her gift. Naomi the pretty pa'e pa'e one."

She's pacing the room now. Waving her hands about. She looks like father. Invoking lightning and wrath and brimstone. I don't know this woman at all. *Did I ever? Do we ever truly know our parents?*

"No," she snaps. "Your father is a good man. When Grandmother died, he didn't have to allow Solomon to come stay with us. He was against it at first. But I begged him. I wanted my son to live with us. I wanted to have him near me. For once. So what if he was grown. So what if he never knew the truth. I knew. He was always mine. I got to have him at last. In my house. In my family. He was such a good boy. Always helpful. Always kind to his sisters. Even

129

when they were naughty. Even when they told lies. For a while I was happy. I had my son." She turns on me and I step back. Instinctive. Bracing for another slap. "But then you had to ruin it."

"I'm your child too," I argue. "The least you could have done is make sure me and my sisters were protected from him. Okay, he was your son, so don't report him. But at least believe me and keep me safe from him. If you'd listened to me the first time I came to you...if you'd only helped me then, I wouldn't have gotten pregnant."

"Why can't you let go of what happened? You're fine," she says. "Michelle was right. You're obsessed. You want everyone to feel sorry for you. Everyone to always be thinking about you, talking about you. No matter how much attention we give you, it's never enough."

Another time, another version of me would have retreated now. Would have believed Mother's every word. But not now. "I'm not fine Mother. Solomon broke me in ways you can't see. He hurt me in ways that don't show on the outside. I've been in therapy for years. I'm thirty years old and I've never had a real boyfriend. Food is my best friend, the only thing that I trust never to let me down, never to betray me. He was a rapist. I told you but you did nothing."

She's covering her ears and shaking her head, and raising her voice to yell, "No. Stop it. I don't want to hear your lies."

"Mother, I can't ever have children." *And that's not just Solomon's fault. It's yours. You condemned me to the rot of an abortion gone wrong and refused to take me to the hospital until it was too late. I'm lucky to be alive.*

She waves that away. It's a triviality. "You're the lucky one," she says. "You have a good life in America. You do what you want. Everything you do is for you. Always selfish. Always thinking of yourself. And you can do that because your father sent you away. We paid a lot of money so you could have a new life. And how do you repay us? By wasting your degree, working at that bakery and living a sinful life." She rushes to add, "Don't try to deny it. I know you do bad things there."

She shakes her fist at me. "I did help you! God forgive me, I did help you. I took you to that woman. You don't understand. You will never know how much my love for you, how much it cost. I should never have taken you to that woman. I broke God's law for you."

"Was it really for me?" I ask. Even though I already know the answer.

"Your father gave me a second chance. I couldn't allow his daughter to be pregnant. His position at the college. All his congregation. How would it look? You were a bad girl and I had to fix it. *Thou shalt not kill.* But for you, I killed an innocent baby and because of that, God punished me. Solomon got cancer because of me." She sinks into a chair and covers her face with her hands, rocking back and forth with a soft keening cry. "He died. He was mine. I held him in my arms like this and he died. He was my baby. My son. He's gone. And it's all my fault. I'm sorry, I'm sorry."

There they are. The words I wanted to hear. Except they aren't for me.

I watch my mother cry for the son I never knew she'd had. All the somber, tortured pictures of Jesus watch too.

There's a sound from the open doorway. Father. How long has he been there? How much has he heard?

He shuffles into the room with his awkward gait, looking incredibly small. Old. And weary.

Stops in front of me. The hoarse whisper. "Forgiveness." For me? For him? For mother?

Then he goes to my mother and sits beside her. One arm on the small of her back as she shakes with grief. A rare show of physical intimacy from this most restrained Samoan of couples.

I walk out with that image and I know with rock sure certainty. I will never come back to this house.

CHAPTER
Nine

I stumble out of the house, on autopilot. *One foot in front of the other. Don't think. Don't feel.* Don't give in to the galu afi wave of rage that will surely kill us all if it's released.

This is the problem with secrets. They're overrated. I have been an unwilling bearer of secrets all my life and resentful of their crushing weight. But now, I wish others had kept their secrets a little better.

It's not simply finding out that Solomon was my brother and not my uncle. It's all of it. That Mother got pregnant when she was underage. To a much older man. And didn't see it as rape. That she sees Solomon's cancer as God's punishment upon her because she took me to have an abortion.

Above all, it's the truth I saw revealed in her eyes. She believed I should have died instead of Solomon. She *wishes* I had died instead. His cancer was an unfair punishment. And every time she looks at me, she is reminded of the son who was taken from her.

I go to Tamarina's house where I sleep all day and all night. Sleep is better than thinking. Than processing all that my mother has revealed. I would sleep through the new day too but the children force me awake.

"Aunty, get up. Your boyfriend is here." A giggle.

Jason Momoa is here?

I struggle awake bleary eyed and musu at being woken. "Go away."

But the children are determined. Rotten brats. Finally it sinks through my miserable haze. Jackson is here. He's brought presents for the babies. For Tamarina.

"He bringed presents for us too!" crows Stella.

I look at the cheerful faces of my nieces and nephews clustered around my bed, their sweaty happiness and simultaneous irritation with each other. Tim as he argues with Tina about his word of the day – again. Demetrius as he tugs at Dana's braids and then when she turns to punch him, he counters with, "Wait! There's a cockroach on your hair." His eruption of cackling laughter as she shrieks and jumps, flailing at her hair and the non-existent insect.

Growing up, I'd always wanted a brother. I'd always been envious of the girls in the village who had brothers. Brothers to look after them, boss them around, pester them, laugh with them. Brothers to get lectured at by every aunty and uncle about honouring their sisters. Brothers who would treat me as the pupil of their eye. A brother who would sing songs to me and my beloved sister-ness, just like

Vaniah Toloa.

Now I know I had a brother. And he had raped me many times over.

Vomit is sudden and surprising. I lurch from the bed and make it to the bathroom just in time, retching into the toilet bowl while the children make loud noises of disgust behind me.

"Ewwww yuck Aunty!"

Except for Stella who is forever caring and concerned. But from a distance. From the doorway she asks timidly, "Aunty Scar, are you gonna die? Please don't die!" There's tears in her voice and I throw her what I hope is a reassuring smile.

"I'm fine. Don't worry."

I'm not sick. But I'm definitely not fine either. I thought I had dealt with this stuff over the years. I thought I was fine with it. The sour taste in my mouth tells me I'm not. I retch and heave again. Another exclamation of combined fascination and repugnance from my audience.

Then, a speculative LOUD voice, "Ooh Aunty Scar, are you pregnant?!"

What the fuck Tina?!

Her twin chimes in. "Yeah, maybe you got a baby

growing in you. Our mum always throws up when she's got babies growing."

This is the problem with having parents who raise you to be woke children. You become pesky nuisances who know too much about everything, *except* about when is the right and wrong time to keep your knowledge to your damn self.

I wipe my hand across my mouth and take a deep breath as I reach up to hit the flush button. "No. I'm not pregnant."

"How can you be sure though?" insists Dana, warming up to this idea of a pregnant Aunty Scar. "Did you have a scanner look inside your tummy? We saw Mum's babies inside her tummy. They had bones like a dinosaur! It was so cool."

"Aunty can we come to your scanner and see your babies and their dinosaur bones?" asks Demetrius eagerly.

"No you can't!" I stumble to my feet and rinse my mouth out in the sink with toothpaste, then turn. That's when I see him. Jackson. Standing in the hall, an inscrutable look on his face. How much did he hear? Wait, does he think what my nosey fiapoto nieces and nephews think?

"Here he is!" exclaims Stella. "Here's your boyfriend Aunty Scar!" The other children giggle and nudge at each other as they stare first at Jackson, then at me, and back again.

I want to die. Then I see Jackson's face. He has a huge grin, a kind of wolf-ish leer as he leans against the doorjamb, not taking his eyes off me once. "Why yes, it's me. Your boyfriend." The way he lingers on the word, sends shivers of delight through me. And the way he looks at me has tendrils of icy fire dancing up my spine. I could stand there all day and let him look at me that way, but then the sniggers and teasing *ooooh's* of our audience remind me where we are. In the bathroom of my sister's house. With a pack of cute but bratty children in here with me.

"Do y'all mind? A little privacy please?" I announce as I herd the children out.

"We were worried about you, Aunty Scar," argues Demetrius with righteous indignation.

"Yes, we don't want you to die Aunty," says Stella in a still-tremulous voice that pierces me with regret.

I drop to my knees to give her a quick hug. "I'm fine baby. I promise. It was just a tummy bug."

"Not any babies?" asks Tim hopefully one more time as he traipses out after the others.

"No! There's no babies in my stomach dammit, okay? Now shoo. Buzz away," I give Jackson what I hope is a blasé eye roll. Like, *can you believe how silly crazy these children are? Ha, kids!*

I follow the children out into the corridor and shut the

bathroom firmly behind me. The last thing Jackson needs right now, is a full frontal of the toilet where I just threw up. It means though that I'm a little too close to him in the narrow hall. Which makes me feel crowded and claustrophobic – as well as excited – at the same time.

"What are you doing here?" I ask, with my face averted because hello, vomit breath.

"Looking for my girlfriend," teases Jackson. He tugs me to him and I go, because when Jackson Emory wants to hold you, that's what you do. You go. You melt. You press against him, every inch of you alive with happiness to be touching him, breathing him, tasting him in the air. His voice is a low growl against my hair as he says my name. Like it's a caress. Like my name is something delicious and divine. That's how Jackson holding me, feels. In his arms, I am delicious and divine. *(My prayer for all of you is that you find yourself a man who makes you feel that way.)*

Delicious and divine.

For a blissful sweet moment I am lost in the sweet joy of him. Then I jerk back to reality. To awareness. "How much of that did you hear? You know those kids are just playing right?"

He lets me pull away, but keeps my hand in his, so our fingers are linked, his other arm leans on the wall behind me, above my head so all I can see and experience, is him. We may be in my sister's house crowded with assorted children, cousins and with the sound of Jacob's busy mechanic shop next door – but here in the dim hallway, we are in our own world. And nothing can break through the shelter that he is.

Jackson is doing something good as he takes a deep breath of me. Dancing a line of light kisses in my hair, along my forehead, beside my ear, on my cheek. A low laugh. "You mean you're not pregnant with our love child?" He's teasing and inviting me to play along with him, but I can't joke about pregnancy. Not now. Not ever. He doesn't pick up on my vibe though. He continues. "You're adorable with those kids, you know that? I feel confident that you're going to be an amazing mother to our love child." Another kiss breathed against the side of my neck, another caress. "The dinosaur love children!" A low laugh. But now I'm not feeling the magic anymore. Because even the shelter that is Jackson Emory can't block out the horror that is the truth of all my family secrets. Because there's one secret left that I haven't told him.

I make a non-committal noise. Not agreeing, not disagreeing. Just being. Just here. Just listening. *Can we please stop talking about children? About pregnancy and babies and my imaginary love child?*

He turns serious, not joking anymore. "Hey, I mean it. I know we're new. Just starting out. But I hope you know you can count on me for anything. To be there for anything. I'd be ready to try and be a good father." A boyish grin and a wink. "Even to a dinosaur baby."

I know he means it and he looks so pleased at the thought of us having an imaginary baby together that a wave of sadness hits me. Call it reality. Call it truth. Call it what you will, but there is nothing that can stand in its path. *This can't work.*

I look up at his face and the sheer perfection of him only reinforces what I know to be true and undeniable. No matter how hard I want it not to be. *Jackson and I can't be together.* Because the truth is that I can't be with anyone right now. I'm not ready or able to be in a relationship of any kind. Not a sexilicious sex-only one. And certainly not one with as much truth and light that Jackson is offering.

I pull away then. Withdrawing in more ways than one. Stepping back from him.

He's puzzled by my sudden retreat. "You feeling okay?"

I nod, look over my shoulder so he'll think I'm worried about being caught by the relatives. "Yeah. All good. I sorta need to go. Shower. Get dressed."

"Sure. I'll wait downstairs. Chill with the kids. I texted you to see if we could have lunch. Maybe go to the beach?"

For a moment I forget my nightmare secrets-reveal session with Mother. "You mean, like a date? Really?"

He grins. Boyish and endearing. "Yes, like a date. Where I ask you out, come pick you up and take you somewhere nice. And we talk and get to know each other."

"Only talk?" I say without thinking.

Something sparks in his dark eyes. Something primal and hungry. Something that tugs deep inside me and has me weak and feeling like there's not enough oxygen in this crowded hallway dammit.

"Talk. And other things," says Jackson. Then he reaches to slip his hand beneath my hair, to clasp my neck and dip my head back so he can claim my mouth with his. A deep, hungry kiss that leaves me gasping. *Someone is thirsty. So thirsty!* I sway and Jackson steadies me. I lean into him for a moment, savouring the scent and feel of him. *Once more. One last time.*

Because even without thinking about it, I've already made my decision. Because was there ever really a chance for us? Especially not now. Again I step back. Free from his embrace. Space. Distance. That's what I need. Room. Escape. That's he needs. He may not know it, but I'm doing him a favour.

I take a deep breath. Steel myself. Appeal to my warrior woman ancestor. The aitu of protection. *Give me strength. Give me courage. Give me resolve.* "Actually, it's probably not a good time, y'know? I'm not feeling well."

He shrugs away his disappointment and flash of confusion. "Sure. The things is, I fly out tomorrow. Something's come up at work that I can't offload on anyone else. If you're feeling better later, then maybe we can grab dinner? But then hey, we're both heading back to Vegas, right?" Unspoken is the promise he wrought from me in a hotel room, *'Say yes Scarlet. Say yes to me…'*

It's a promise I won't keep.

"Sure," I say. "I'll call you later and let you know how I feel." Lies.

We say goodbye and I watch from the window as he drives away. Then I'm on the phone changing tickets and making the necessary arrangements. Within a few hours it's all sorted. I'm going back to Vegas. Tamarina gives me a questioning look but doesn't pry. She's always been able to calculate the answers without even asking the question. I'm sorry to be leaving so soon after she's come home with new babies but she waves aside my guilt. "Don't be silly. Jacob's home. And his mum always comes to stay for a few months when we have babies." She says that with tired happiness because Jacob has the blessing of a mother who isn't like ours. My big sister guilty conscience somewhat assuaged, I pack and then head out.

There's only one other person I need to say goodbye to and I know just where to find her.

Aunty Filomena goes to Bingo religiously every Saturday afternoon. Which is perfect because it means I don't have to go back to the house. I don't have to risk seeing my parents.

The hall is a bustling, crowded place, children playing outside under the mango trees as their parents chase luck and fortune inside. I find Aunty at her usual table and slip into the seat beside her. She's surprised and even more so when I whisper my news.

She is sad, but accepting. How much did she hear from the confrontation with Mother? How much does she know?

"When will you come back?" she asks. Because of course I will come back. I'm a daughter of Samoa after all and like the toloa bird, it doesn't matter how far away we fly, or for how long, but we always come back to our familiar nest of water. *Don't we?*

In that moment I notice what I haven't seen before. Aunty Filomena is old. The knowledge is like a punch to my chest. When did it happen? Why hadn't I noticed it before? Does our love for our elders blind us to their mortality? Do we think that like the Tooth Fairy or Santa Claus, that if we just believe hard enough, and not question enough – that they will live forever? And never leave us? Fear claws its way up from my gut, cold and hungry. Why had I not considered it? I am taken back to the day I was first sent away. Aunty Filomena's tears, the comfort of her embrace. It never even occurred to me then that I might not see her again. Had she been thinking of it? Then when I was allowed to return for my 21st, only to be sent packing in disgrace, again – Aunty Filomena had again been the one who accompanied me to the airport with the boy cousins. She had cried that day too. And held me a long time. But again, like the self-obsession of youth, or its inability to comprehend endings – I didn't think it might be the last time.

But today, I see it. Today, I know it. I acknowledge here and now in this sweaty crowd with its overarching smell of too much Impulse and Lynx deodorant, that I might not see Aunty Filomena again.

I hug her fiercely. Feeling the bony frailty of her through the floral mu'umu'u. There's strength and resilience in that frailty, and love. So much love. Tears choke me as I whisper, "One day. I'll come back. I promise." Feeling sick with guilt because I don't mean it.

Because I know she means, when will I come back to the family house, to the aiga, to live with my parents, to be a good daughter. Because always, Aunty Filomena hoped for the best outcomes, for the best of people and the relationships we have with them. Even my parents. She hopes the best of them and that makes me resentful because the little hurt child in me wants her to choose a side, hate them, condemn them. Give up on them. But I know she won't. Because that's not how Aunty Filomena loves.

We don't say that we love each other. Because we are Samoan after all. I want to say thank you for all the years of making my favorite foods. All the times she saw my hurt and tried to heal it the best way she knew how. I want to tell her that I know how much she gave up to be our second mother. That her sacrifice didn't go unnoticed or unappreciated.

Instead, Aunty pats me on the back and repeats the mantra that has sustained me throughout my years of exile.

"Be a good girl Scar. You a good girl. Don't forget, eh?"

I nod. Tell her that I'll remember. *I'm a good girl.*

But today, I try something different. I look her in the eyes and say, "You too Aunty. You be a good girl. Don't forget, eh!"

She's surprised and puzzled for a moment and then she laughs, swats at me with a light hand. "You funny girl. Go on. Don't go too long eh? You come back soon. Now you go. I'm going to miss my Bingo. Alu loa."

I look over my shoulder one more time to see Aunty, trying to memorise her like this, in her element. She is arguing with another woman about the Bingo numbers. Even though she's younger and bigger than Aunty Filomena, it's clear who is winning this confrontation. The other woman doesn't have a prayer of outplaying or out-arguing my aunty. Filomena is happy and ferocious at the same time. Shaking her fist across the room, hurling insults and automatically looking around for stones to throw at people – even though she's in the church hall.

Goodbye Aunty. Ou te alofa ia te oe.

I am on a plane that night. I leave a letter for Jackson. Because I'm not a total bitch. He deserves to know why I can't do it. He doesn't need to be burdened by all the gory details, but I give him the bare bones. I tell him that I'm sorry but I can't say yes. Because I have shit to work through before I can trust anyone enough to let them in.

If we don't fix our brokenness, then we will break others. If nothing else I have learnt that from my parents on this trip home.

I'm sad but I'm also relieved. There's no more secrets

now. I am traversing from Pulotu to the light. I don't know what the future holds and it's scary not knowing, but the lightness of being, of being freed from secrets – it's worth the fear of the unknown.

My name is Scarlet Pele Thompson. I had a brother who betrayed the feagaiga covenant. I hid in shame and darkness, but no longer. I was broken but now I am putting the pieces of me together. I was a prisoner of shame and guilt, but now I am free. I had secrets, I lived with lies – mine and the lies of others, but no more. I walk in truth now. No matter how harsh, brutal or unforgiving the light may be. I'm ready.

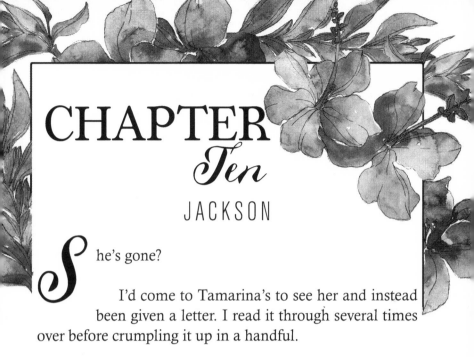

CHAPTER
Ten

JACKSON

*S*he's gone?

I'd come to Tamarina's to see her and instead been given a letter. I read it through several times over before crumpling it up in a handful.

Fuck!

Her rejection is a freight train out of nowhere. How could this happen? Just yesterday she had lain in my arms, that amazing waterfall of hair spread out over the pillow, looking up at me with nothing but trust and happiness in her eyes. Or what I thought was happiness. Turns out I was wrong. She'd said yes. To me, to us. She'd said it with her body many times over. And whispered it to me in the shadows throughout the two most incredible nights of my life. But she'd lied.

'I'm sorry Jackson. You've given me the best days of my life and I wanted so badly to continue on this journey with you. I thought that I could. I thought that I was ready. But I was wrong. There's too much baggage that I haven't fully dealt with. There's too much I haven't told you, and I don't know if I ever could. You deserve to be with someone who can give you the truth. Who can

give you everything. I really wanted to be that person but I can't. Please forgive me.'

Everyone knows what that's code for. What those excuses really mean. *It's not you, it's me.* Ha. It's the classic breakup line known to man. The biggest fucking lie. She couldn't even give me the truth. Not even now. A memory is a knife-stab to the gut. The first day we met. She lied to me then. And in spite of everything we've gone through together over the last few weeks, she's still lying? To herself? To me? Why?

There had been a moment when she stepped out from behind the walls she'd carefully constructed to keep herself safe. That day in the church when she'd told me about being an abuse survivor. No lies. No holding back. No family barriers. Just raw truth. Just us. She'd let me in, let me see her vulnerability and her incredible strength. I think that's the day I started falling for her. Or maybe it was the moment she spilled out of her red dress at the wedding. The flash of her glorious smile when she realised it, her forever ability to laugh at herself, to find gleeful joy in life's moments of realness. A rush of memories. Scarlet and I dancing while her aunties ogled my backside and she tried and failed not to laugh. Scarlet on stage, wearing an octopus corset and singing her heart out. The way her nieces and nephews adore her, hanging on her every word.

I want to smash things. I want – no I need – to get out of here.

There's a sound behind me. A man enters the kitchen.

He's huge. Tall and built like a football player – but none of the bulk is padding. Just muscle. He doesn't smile.

"You're the one who took my wife to the hospital?" he says, accusatory. Still no smile.

"Yes," I say. "Jackson. You must be Jacob." I extend my hand. I have no smiles in me either but I can be polite.

The man ignores my hand. Instead he takes several steps forward and grabs me. Its crushing and terrifying because for a crazy moment I'm not sure if this is a hug, or he's trying to kill me.

"Thank you uso," he says, with muffled emotion. "You saved my wife and my children."

I'm having trouble breathing so I just bring a hand up and pat him on the back.

Thankfully Tamarina walks in just then. "Jacob I think you're choking him. You can let him go now."

The man releases me and I can breathe again. "I didn't do anything," I say. "It was your wife who did all the work. Basically we just stood there and tried not to get in her way. Tamarina was amazing."

Jacob's face lights up in a smile as he looks at his wife. It's a smile that completely transforms him. "She is amazing," he agrees. Then back to me, "But she told me what happened. You took care of her and the babies. I owe you a debt I can never repay."

His face is granite seriousness again and I don't know how to respond. I'm not going to say 'it was nothing', because it's starkly obvious that to Jacob, his family means everything.

Tamarina steps into the silence. "Jacob wants to name the babies after you and Scarlet."

"What?!"

Jacob nods solemnly. "The girls will be called Jackson and Scarlet."

I'm stunned. I try to protest. "But you don't really even know me?"

Jacob speaks. "Tamarina says you are a good man. My wife is an excellent judge of character. It will be an honor for our child to bear your name."

"No that's not necessary. Really. I was happy to help. Besides, what kind of name is Jackson for a girl? She'll grow up hating her namesake."

Tamarina waves away my excuses. "She'll love it. Don't worry. It's tradition in Samoa to name children after the day they were born, or after a person who was significant in their delivery." She teases, "Hey, it's either you or the doctor who was on duty that night and the doctor's name was Peiosepua'a! Which means 'Looks like a pig'...so

Jackson is much better."

We all laugh and the mood lightens considerably. But inside I am chaos. With a name, they are binding me to their family and I know after my time here in Samoa - that's not a small thing. The ties of family come with boundless alofa and generosity. But they also bring responsibility and obligations. Am I worthy of that? And do I want to be? Scarlet just dumped me. Took my hopes of an actual relationship with her – and stomped all over them. Don't I want to just get on a plane and go as far away as possible from this country, from this aiga, from everything that's connected to the woman who I thought I was falling in love with? And never look back? But what can I do? Tell them I refuse to allow their baby to be named Jackson? Offend the aiga who have been nothing but kind and welcoming to me? It's not like I own the copyright for a name…

We small-talk for a while and then Jacob has to go back to work so he shakes my hand with a wincingly firm grip. "You are family now," he says to me. "If you ever need anything, just ask."

I'm about to leave too when Tamarina stops me. "You got Scarlet's letter?"

I nod, and try to keep the bitterness out of my voice. "Yeah. Not that it said much."

"You care about her, don't you."

"It's that obvious, huh?" I say with a lightness that I

don't feel.

Tamarina looks at me for a long moment, with an inscrutable air. Most people don't stare at you when you can see it. Scarlet's youngest sister doesn't hide when she's studying you. She has an unflinching gaze that unsettles you when you first meet her. But I'm used to it now. And after being all up in a woman's business, trying to help when she's giving birth in the backseat of car? Well, it kind of dispels any walls you may have had with each other!

"My sister feels things deeply," says Tamarina. A frown. "Even when logic dictates one path? She has emotions that take her down another. It doesn't always make sense. Not to me anyway."

I don't know where this conversation is going or what Tamarina is trying to tell me. So I nod with what I hope is polite interest.

Tamarina goes to a desk in the corner and rifles through a drawer, then comes to me with a photograph. It's of three little girls sitting in a frangipani tree, grinning at the camera. Sisters. She doesn't have to tell me which one is Scarlet. I know her immediately. A wild tangle of hair, deep-set dark eyes, and a huge smile that shows the slight gap between her two front teeth. She's obviously darker than her two sisters, and bigger, bolder. She radiates an open kind of cheerful joy that is unafraid and unrestrained. It's a free spiritedness that I have only caught glimpses of in the adult Scarlet. When we're alone, away from her family and the rest of the outside world, and she laughs with that belly-deep pleasure.

When she's with her nieces and nephews, telling them a story, refereeing their squabbles and she's trying to be the serious disciplinarian, but failing. That night at the club when she took to the stage with Beyonce and belted out their anthem of independence, when she was strutting the stage in her octopus costume.

"That's what she was like. Before. The toughest girl in the neighbourhood and so funny," says Tamarina. "Everyone wanted to be on her team in all the games. Everyone looked to her for the ideas, to make the plans. She was the boss. So confident. Always so creative and organising all the cousins to do skits, tell stories, and act out our favorite movies. And she loved to dance. Her and Beyonce watched music videos religiously and learned all the moves." Tamarina smiles then at the memory. "But above all that, Scar valued her role as our big sister. She took care of me and Naomi. I was different from the other kids. But nobody teased me because if they did, Scar would make them stop. She was always protecting us. Covering for us. Watching out for us." She points to the tree in the photograph. "Naomi fell out of this same frangipani tree and broke her arm. This was after Scar told her not to climb up by herself and Naomi didn't listen. I'm the one who dared her that she couldn't reach the top branches. But Scar never said anything when Mother got angry at her for not looking after Naomi properly. Mother used the salu on her and Scar just stood there with her head bowed. Because she believed it was her fault. Because she didn't want me to get in trouble too."

It's the most words I've heard Tamarina speak in one go. I don't say anything or even move because I'm worried it will freak her out and make her stop.

Tamarina frowns then. "Things changed when Solomon came. I didn't understand why. Not then. There were many whispers that I couldn't make sense of. My big sister changed. Slowly. And then they sent her to America. I could see she didn't want to go. She didn't want to leave us. She felt responsible." She takes a deep breath and looks at me. "We all carry secrets inside us. Scar has more than most people. The man who loves my sister, will need to be patient. He has to be a good man and know how to love, like my Jacob knows how to love. He will need to be strong and endure with enough hope for two. But whoever that man is, he will be a lucky man because my sister knows how to love. She is loyal. Protective. She takes care of those she cares about. No matter what." Her eyes get laser beam intense. "If that man knows he can't be that? Can't love my sister like that? Then he should leave her alone."

Warning received loud and clear.

From somewhere in the house, a baby's mewling cry is heard. Tamarina sighs and her scary laser eyes now just look tired. "I must go." At the door, she pauses. "I have seen how Scarlet is when she's with you. She is happy. No matter what she wrote in her letter? You make her happy."

154

CHAPTER
Eleven

SCARLET

*N*ina meets me at the airport. It's easy to find her in the crowd. She's the breathtaking statuesque supermodel radiating sensuality and *don't-you-wish-you-could-be-me* confidence. Even in stiletto heels, and a demure pencil skirt, she glides through the waiting area, grace personified.

Nina has different personas for different occasions and today she is in executive CEO mode. Cinched waist jacket with a hint of cleavage, hair pulled back in a simple chignon at the nape of her neck, a silver torque necklace, subdued makeup with just a splash of red at the lips, and severe glasses. The suave composure cracks though when she catches sight of me, as she quickens her step with a huge smile on her face. We air kiss and hug, but only for a brief moment because she knows I don't like too much of that stuff.

I have prepped myself on the long flight, to show her the best side of me. I'm not ready to talk about the gut wrenching revelations and the messy family dynamics. Or the glory (and pain) of Jackson.

So I have a smile and a litany of funny stories ready for her as we make our way to the car. But once we get to the apartment and we've lugged my bags up the stairs because the elevator is on the blink again, Nina confronts me with her hands on her hips.

"What happened?" she says.

I avoid her searching gaze. From experience, I know its near impossible to lie to Nina. I busy myself with turning the air conditioning on and grabbing a soda from the fridge.

"What do you mean? I've been telling you about my trip ever since we got in the car."

"No," she says abruptly with that no-nonsense tone of hers. The one she uses on slow-moving cocktail waiters. "Something happened over there. I know it. Something bad." She studies me some more and then her eyes widen. "And something really good."

"Yeah, I survived being with my dysfunctional family. That's good."

"You met someone," Nina announces with triumph. "Someone hot and sexy as fuck!"

For a moment I am transported to a grey-toned beach day with Jackson. I feel the steel edge of the car at my back as he kisses me, the razor edge of his cheek against my skin. I hear the cry of white terns as we make love under a green mantle of tropical forest. I see his smile, the slight dimple in his left cheek, the dark promise in his eyes when he's teasing me.

"Yes, I did," I confess.

And then I burst into tears.

Nina hugs me. Screw the rules on Scarlet's #dontTouchMe hangups. I cry for what seems like forever. All the hurt of the last few days rushes out, impossible to hold back any longer. My best friend hugs me and when enough time has passed, she sits me up.

"What did the asshole do to you?" There's menace in her eyes. My bestie is ready to kill for me. "What happened?"

"No, it wasn't like that. It wasn't him. He was perfect. It was me and my shitty family." I erupt into sobs again. Straight up bawling. The kind like when you're a kid and you're hiccupping and your crying is caught in an endless repeat frame and you're making no sense any more.

Nina can see that only the best damage control can have a hope of bringing any solace here. She goes to the kitchen and brings back an arsenal of weapons, lining them up on the table in front of me.

A tub of ice cream. Rum'n'raisin, my favorite.

A takeaway container with half a chocolate banana cream pie.

A bottle of champagne.

"What's all this?" The confusion at least puts a dent in my crying fit. "How did you know I'd need it?"

She shrugs. "I got it for something else. Never mind what. Now, eat and talk. Tell me everything."

Two scoops of ice cream, a bite of pie and I'm ready to talk. I tell her everything. All the bad. All the good. All the ugly. I hold nothing back. The shadows lengthen as the day fades and still I talk. Nina is the best listener and because she knows all my sordid past, she is able to connect all the dots without my needing to rehash anything.

"I'm sorry Scarlet," she says when I'm done. There's a razor edge of anger in her voice. "I wish I could have a few words with your parents. Just give me fifteen minutes in a room with that woman who doesn't deserve to call herself a mother. And that man who dares to claim he's a Christian!" She takes a deep breath to collect herself. "Sorry, I know they're your parents but screw them Scarlet. I thought I had bad parents, but yours are in a whole other next level of fuckery."

I can't argue with her. Even though my Samoan soul cringes at anyone putting my parents and the F-word in the same sentence. Because no matter what parents do to us, we're supposed to honor them. (If we want to live long on this earth anyway. The Bible says so.) Nina sees my discomfort and she's known me long enough to understand it. Even though she doesn't agree with it.

"Right, enough about that. I want more about Jackson."

She wants to see pictures. Of Jackson. The wedding. Of Brian the photographer. Of me in my emerald dress (that she chose for me). Of me in my scarlet corset dress (that she bought for me). Of me in my maillot (that she ordered for me). She frowns when she sees me wearing it with shorts and a lavalava, but takes pity on me thanks to my tears, and doesn't hassle me like I know she is dying to.

"So how did you end it with Jackson?" she wants to know. "What did you tell him?"

"I didn't tell him anything. I wrote him a letter."

"You did what?"

"There was too much going on with my family and I'm a mess so I wrote him a letter," I say.

"And what did this letter say?" Nina has one eyebrow raised. Like the Rock, only scarier. Because Nina in boss-mode, is more frightening than the Rock could ever be.

"Just that I enjoyed spending time with him and he's a great person. But at this point in my life I can't commit to a serious relationship. I've got issues to deal with, and I hope he has a safe trip back home."

"That's it?" says Nina in disbelief. "The man gives you four orgasms in one night, and all you can say is – *have a safe trip home*?!"

This is the problem with telling Nina everything. She remembers details you would rather she didn't, and then she repeats them out loud. Really loud.

"It's for the best," I say. "It would never have worked."

"Why not?"

"Because we come from different worlds." It sounds pathetic, even to me.

"Yes, because you're an alien from Mars," Nina says drily. "Try another one."

"He doesn't really know me. It was a holiday fling. That's why it worked, why we connected so well."

A sly grin then. "Mmmhmmm, girl you got that right. You connected again, and again, and again!" She says it with a breathy sex-filled voice which has me rolling my eyes and for a brief moment we laugh.

Then she gets serious again. "That doesn't make sense either. Sounds like you let him know more about you than you've ever told any other man. I mean, who else besides me knows about your past? About all of it? You told this honey, about the most painful things and showed him your scars."

"Well not quite," I say, thinking of what I didn't tell him as the light streamed through the stained glass window of the Virgin Mary and baby Jesus.

Nina waves away my disclaimers. "No. I won't let you do this. Do you know how rare and precious it is to find someone you can show your true self to – and have him accept you in all your complicated, unique hot mess, as you are? What I would give to have that."

There's anger in her voice now. And pain. I catch the gleam of unshed tears in her eyes and a gut-punch of guilt shames me.

"Oh Nina, I'm sorry. I wasn't thinking, I didn't mean…"

"It's okay. It's not about me and my shit." She takes a deep breath, steels herself and for a moment there is silence.

"How's Andrew?" I ask. Andrew is her on-again-off-again boyfriend, a marketing executive she met at the club where she works weekends.

"There is no more Andrew," she says with a curl to her lip. "I pushed too hard for him to introduce me to his friends and he ended it. Said we weren't compatible. He sure seemed happy with our compatibility though, when he was banging me on every durable surface in this apartment."

I have a flash image of them having sex on the table we're eating ice cream on and I jump up, holding my bowl aloft. "Ewww yuck Nina! Germs."

"Ah stop panicking. I cleaned! Disinfected the whole place for two days straight while you were gone. Therapy."

Nina's a clean freak and forever on my case to raise my hygiene standards to hers, so somewhat mollified, I gingerly sit back down. But still. Who's going to disinfect my brain from the pictures of them going at it on our dining table?

"I don't want to talk about Andrew," she says firmly. "He's in the past. Forget him. We're talking about you and your issues and how you put up walls so that a hot honey like Jackson can't reach you."

"Fine, we won't talk about Andrew." I go over and give her a quick hug. "But let me just say this. He's an asshole. He was never worthy of a woman like you. And any man who can't handle everything that you are? Doesn't deserve to even be in the same room as you, let alone banging you in our apartment. That special man who is worthy? He is out there, looking for you. And one day, he'll find you and treasure and adore you the way you should be treasured."

For a moment Nina shows me the vulnerable jelly vulnerability she is inside. "You think so?"

"I know so."

She gives me a wobbly smile and for a moment we are freshmen in college again…

My first day moving into the dorm, terrified and trying not to show it. Feeling like an imposter with my full scholarship , still uncertain how I ended up there in an Ivy League school. Slowly unpacking my suitcase and then hearing raised voices from across the hall. *Only the first day and already people are fighting?* The noise got louder and impossible to ignore. It brought a growing crowd of spectators and even I paused in my unpacking to look out at the two roomies yelling at each other. One was a petite white girl with a blonde bob, her face twisted in distaste. The other was a black fa'afafine dressed like she just stepped out of VOGUE magazine. Red dress with knee high boots, flawless makeup.

It didn't take a genius to figure out what they were fighting about, as the beautiful faafafine said with barely contained rage, "This is a co-ed dorm."

The blonde raised her voice, in a heavy southern accent. "Aah know that. And aah asked to room with a girl."

"I am a girl."

"No you aint. You're a big black man wearing a dress. And it don't matter if it's Chanel, you're still not a girl and aah am not sleepin' in the same room as you, getting undressed with you watching me!"

"Oh please, even if I were into girls, you are not my type. You have nothing that I want," the other said icily. "And besides, I refuse to room with a transphobic racist."

The blonde girl spluttered at that. "Who aah you calling racist? How dare you? Aah am not racist. Aaah have black friends. Black FEMALE friends."

"Now you're going to try the I-have-one-black-friend-so-that-excuses-my-racist-ass card? Oh that's tired. And weak. I'm out of here. I'm going to file a complaint with the office. We'll see how this goes down."

"That's right, you go!" The girl lost it then. "Aah guarantee you nobody here wants to room with the likes of you." She gesticulated wildly at the small crowd that had gathered in the corridor. "None of them will room with you. It's a safety issue. There's no room for you here!"

The fa'afafine seemed to finally be aware of the audience. She looked around and I caught a brief flicker of panic as she let her mask of confidence slip. It was only an instant but it was enough.

"You can room with me." My voice was a squeak and I had to repeat myself louder to be heard.

Everyone turned to look. The blonde paused in her tirade and I said to her, "I can switch with you." Then to the faafafine. "Only if you want to. It's just a suggestion."

There was a tense moment where I died a thousand deaths, quailing inside as everyone stared. The fa'afafine glared at me, and for a wild minute I was sure she would reject my offer. Reject me. But then she squared her shoulders and bestowed a brilliant smile on me, with her hand outstretched.

"Thank you," she said, "I'm Nina."

The blonde girl packed up her bags (with sniffs of

disdain) and I moved to the other room. I was making up my bed with the elei bedspread the Aunties had sent me to college with when Nina confronted me. Once the crowd had dispersed (the show all over) and the door was securely closed against all faikakala's.

"Why?" Arms crossed across her abundant chest. "Why'd you offer to switch?"

I shrugged. "I didn't like the look of my roomie."

She didn't buy it. But I wasn't about to try and give her the entire low-down on Samoa's third gender and the cultural identity of Faafafine and Faatama. So instead I pulled out the framed photo of me and Beyonce that I'd brought to put on my desk. "This is my cousin Beyonce. We grew up together and went to school together too."

It was enough.

It didn't take long for Nina and I to become the kind of friends who stay up until two in the morning, talking about anything and everything. We were oceans apart in many ways, but soul sisters in others. Her family made mine look almost angelic in comparison. She only had one sibling – an older brother that she loved fiercely. He had stood by her when her parents threw her out. Nina had told them she was going to transition and her father had beaten her, breaking ribs and affecting her hearing in one ear. Her mother had stood there praying through the ordeal. Nina's brother Adam had called the police which probably saved her life but Nina refused to press charges. Instead she had taken a scholarship at a college as far away as possible from home. I told her about Beyonce and the other fa'afafine I knew back home and she had been wistful.

"It's not all roses," I warned. "Beyonce will tell you how hypocritical it can be. Her family relies on her as the main income earner and they're very proud of her position at the bank. They even cheer on her performances at the club. But that's where it ends. She has to hide her relationships from them. It's like, you can be faafafine but you just can't have sex with a man." I added wryly, "Although many men have no problem with having sex with faafafine. They just won't acknowledge them in public."

Nina knew all about that. Cue Andrew. Who had been preceded by a long line of lovers with the same aversion to dating her publicly. Nina's family had cut her off financially and she'd had to work her way through college. Which is how she'd started in the exotic dancer business. She'd since moved to being a showgirl in a cabaret show. She worked five days at an accountancy firm in the city, but her real income earner was show-girling.

We bonded over our fractured families and shared hurts. We knew first-hand that the people who love us are the ones who hurt us the deepest because we let them. Because we care. Because they know all our vulnerabilities and our flaws.

But Nina was also different in the ways that made our friendship richer. While I hid my insecurities with food, she dressed hers up in an impeccable sense of style and a cloak of professional confidence. Her razor sharp intellect combined with her street smarts made her the perfect advisor in all things. And she had an intuitiveness that I lacked.

She's the one who first pointed out what I had missed about my aunties. She only needed to come home for toonai with me once and on the drive back to the apartment she said, "It's so sweet to see them still so in love. I want that."

"What are you talking about?" had been my befuddled response.

"I want to be seventy years old and still in love, and have my lover look at me the way they look at each other," she sighed.

WTF?? "What are you saying about my aunts?"

It was her turn to be confused. "What do you mean?" Then as comprehension dawned on her, "You don't know? Are you kidding me? How long have you lived with them?!"

"I don't know what you're on about. My aunts are sisters who live together…" I trailed away as I realised that wasn't true. I'd seen their passports, I'd helped fill in forms for them numerous times. They had different last names and I knew they had different parents. But I'd always assumed that like all the rest of my "aunties" in Samoa, they were cousins or some kind of aiga.

"They're aiga," I said feebly, even as I knew my words to be false. And then in a rush of memory so many details over the ten years that I'd lived with them all clicked into place. They shared the same bedroom and the same bed. *But everyone in Samoa shares beds and living space…* is what I'd always thought so I'd thought nothing of it. The time Aunty Amalia had been rushed to hospital with a burst appendix. Aunty Mareta weeping by her bedside, clutching her hand, brushing her hair with tenderness. The love in the room a palpable thing you could reach out and hold it in the palm of your hand.

Nina had laughed all the way home, and it was still something she loved to tease me about. Of course once I'd had it pointed out to me, it was all I could see and I didn't know how I had missed it all these years. My aunts were wholly and completely in love. Is that why they moved away from Samoa I wondered? Did the rest of the aiga know? Mother must be clueless about their relationship because otherwise she would have said something about it long before this. Father wouldn't have sent me to live with the aunties if he'd known they were lesbians. Would he?

Back in the present, the shadows lengthen and Nina can see she isn't going to be changing my mind any time soon about breaking up with Jackson.

"I'm not ready," I say sadly. "I want to be. But finding out this stuff from Naomi and my parents? I thought I'd sorted all my shit out, y'know? But this hit me hard and dragged up all kinds of stuff that I thought I'd fixed a long time ago. I can't be in a relationship right now."

Because she knows me. Because she loves me, Nina doesn't argue. "Okay. I get why you shouldn't be in a relationship with anyone right now. Not even an incredibly hot man like Jason Momoa's twin brother. Promise me you'll go back to therapy and talk through the new developments on the fucked up parents front? I'll call and make the appointment with Dr Franklin if you don't!"

I shake my head and laugh, "I'm perfectly capable of calling the therapist myself thank you very much."

Nina has to try one more time though, "Couldn't you have no-strings-attached sex with Jackson though? In the meantime. Until you sort your shit out?" A laugh and then she gets serious again, giving me a searching look, with her head tilted to one side. "You're not the same person who went to Samoa Scarlet. I'm not quite sure how or in what ways you've changed, but I'm excited to find out."

CHAPTER
Twelve

*F*orgiveness.

I've thought a lot about my father's last word to me. I've asked myself, how can that possibly be an answer, a solution to anything? It's made me angry. The trite failure of such a word to fully absolve a lifetime of shame, guilt and fear. Erase the wrongs that have been done. Make everything new again.

No. Impossible.

Forgive he who hurt me? Forgive she who ignored my plea for help? Forgive he who was blind and deaf to it all, because he was too busy saving souls? (Or as it turns out, he was also too busy with acting on his Biblically lustful adulterous heart!?) Forgive the woman whose bacteria-ridden hands took away a thousand possibilities for cheeky grins like Stella's, sticky kisses and hugs like Tim's, for a belly that swells with hopeful anticipation? Forgive the cutting words and sideways glances, the suffocating judgement that played its part in everyone's choices?

No. That's too many. Too much for one word to handle.

Instead, I seek to forgive two only.

Me.

You are not to blame. You were a child. You did nothing to cause it. You were not responsible. You are innocent. There were those charged with your safety and wellbeing. They were remiss in their responsibility and they will bear that. *'Better that a millstone be hung around their necks so they drown in the depths of the sea, than they should harm a hair on the head of any of my children.'*

And God.

Sacrilege I know. For who am I to forgive God? Is God not above reproach? Beyond my reach? I am imperfect. My mortality is but the whisper of an eyelash in the face of eternity that God is. But I cannot accept God as some vengeful spiteful being who metes out wrath and extracts penance. He doesn't block suitable husbands from single women who should be home taking care of their aged parents. He doesn't send cancer to sexual predators. Or punish fourteen year olds who have abortions. God doesn't demand an eye for an eye. The life of my mother's son for the unborn baby of her daughter.

And it's not God's fault that I was raped.

I have hated God for what was done to me. For not saving me. For not striking Solomon down with the lightning strike of righteous judgement. For allowing hypocrisy to flower, scarlet fields of unchecked poppy rot, in our home, and within the leader of our congregation. I have borne this hatred for too long and it's time to lay it down.

171

Because, maybe God isn't as omniscient as we imagine he is. Maybe he doesn't see all. Know all. Maybe God doesn't build walls and cast sinners into outer darkness. Thunder from pulpits and call down fire and brimstone on scarlet whores.

Maybe God is not what Father proclaimed himself to be. Maybe God isn't what Mother believed him to be.

I wonder, maybe God is like Aunty Filomena. One who loves unselfishly, without compromise. With her whole heart. One who hopes all things for you. Makes you koko rice and pineapple pie when you are sad. Throws stones at taxi drivers who are rude about you. She weeps when you hurt, when she can't shelter you from all that would harm you. Maybe God believes the best of you, through all things. When you screw up, there is hurt and sadness in her eyes, but more than that, there is reassurance that yes, you can pick yourself up and keep going. You can try again. You can move forward. You can let go.

Because maybe like Aunty Filomena, God lets go. Of our shortcomings and imperfections. But she never lets go of us. Instead, She holds you in her arms and whispers, *'Be a good girl. Be strong.'*

Forgive? It's taken me a long time. But yes I forgive.

It's fragile. A dusting of kapok in the wind. Who knows

where it will go, if it will last? But it's a seed. And in seeds, there are untold possibilities.

For now that's enough.

CHAPTER
Thirteen

*I*t's my first day back at work and it's a welcome relief to be in my comfort zone, my happy place. I stand there for a few minutes breathing in deeply of the familiar – vanilla, cinnamon, the bite of chili, the possibilities in the smell of rising yeasty dough, the delight of buttercream, maple sugar and pecans, cocoa and caramelized sugar, chocolate and orange ganache, the bubbling of peaches on the stove for a fresh batch of pies. Every delicious aroma is all the more clear because I know there's a deadline now on how long I'll be here to savor them.

"You missed us, didn't you?" says Anna as she gives me a quick hug. Brisk and brusque, she steps back and gives me an appraising look. "But you're not staying long." It's not a question and I'm caught by surprise.

"What do you mean?"

She shakes her head, a half-grin on her face and hands on her hips. "You're leaving us. Finally."

I gape at her. "Who told you?"

"Nobody. I could see it as soon as you walked in that

door," she says.

I stumble over my words apologetic and not making much sense. She stops me with one hand up. "Scarlet, you weren't supposed to work here forever. When you first came here for a job, it was meant to be temporary. You're not a baker. You've got a few skills, but this isn't your life's work."

Her matter of factness bruises my baking pride. "It could be. I didn't realize that you weren't happy with my work." *I've got baking skills dammit!*

She waves away my protests with her usual brusqueness. "Ah stop it. You do fine and you know you're a great employee. But answer me this – does the bakery give you joy? Well, does it?"

I give her a rueful grin and shrug. "Eating your custard pies does?"

"See? Life is too short to waste on that which doesn't give you joy. We all have to do things we don't want to sometimes. A girl's gotta eat and survive! But then, survival mode should only ever be temporary. Not forever. A stepping stone to something else, something better. The bakery was always my dream. This is my passion. What's yours? I hope you're quitting to do something that gets you closer to your dream."

"Actually yes, I am. I've been writing novels under a pen name. Sales are good and I'm quitting the bakery so I can write fulltime." She's only the second person I've told of my new decision. It feels good to speak the words out loud and give them realness with every time I say it.

Anna beams at me. "That's excellent news. What kind of books do you write?"

"Romance. Trash books," I say apologetically, steeling myself for the dismissive sneer that romance often gets.

Anna's face lights up. "My favorite! You bring me some of your books before you leave. Your going away present for your boss. The best boss you ever had."

I am doubtful. "Umm, they're a little...racey. Y'know, sexy."

"The more sex the better," says Anna. "I've read Fifty Shades of Grey eight times. Me and Boris are always looking for inspiration in the bedroom."

And with that she stalks back into the kitchen, barking over her shoulder, "Take care of the customers. Hurry."

Okay then. I guess Anna won't be devastated to see me leave! I have to smile though as I grab an apron and head out to the front. Because Anna's right. Life is too short to waste on that which doesn't give us joy, and thinking about my latest novel work in progress back at the apartment, I have joy waiting for me.

My smile lasts only as long as it takes to see what customer is waiting at the counter.

Fuck.

Kevin gives me a huge smile. "Look who's back! Scarlet baby, I missed you. Sandra doesn't offer the same great view when she's boxing up my order."

From across the room Sandra mutters acidly, "You mean Sandra doesn't put up with your shit like Scarlet does." We exchange looks of shared disgust.

Kevin ignores her as he leans on the counter so he's at eye level with my chest, making an appreciative *HMMMM* noise. "A dozen of my usual sweet buns honey. And a coffee. With extra sugar and cream."

He keeps up the commentary as I make his coffee and pack buns into the box. He's ladling on the praise today as if to make up for weeks of my having a break from his sexual favor. My eyes are *deep pools of mystery* and my *'island lusciousness'* adds extra spice to his morning.

He asks, "Did you put on weight on your Saamowah holiday? In all the right places?" (A leer.) Because he says my uniform is looking extra snug and inviting today. When I turn to grab him extra napkins, he compliments my ass. 'So much to hang on to! Ha, ha. Are all the island women back in your country as curvey and delicious as you?"

I plaster a polite smile on my face as I give him his order, wishing for him to just hurry up and leave now. *Get the hell out of here.* I'm cutting a piece of carrot cake for another customer. But he's not done. He gets a five dollar note from his wallet and reaches across to tuck it into my top, casual and possessive. "Here you go babe, a tip. Always a pleasure seeing you." And then his hand pat-brushes my breast. No accident, no apology.

I freeze. Sandra's hiss of shock from somewhere behind me is the only sound in the bakery in what seems like an endless moment. My vision blurs . Is it rage? Or fear? Or both? I only have one clear thought stamped in my mind, like a flashing billboard that won't be ignored.

Aunty Pativaine was right. I need a sapelu.

I stare across the counter at this man who has plagued my every working week since I started at the bakery. The smirk on his pasty face. Every time the sight of him sent my stomach into a tail spin of dread. Aunty Pativaine wouldn't put up with his shit. She wouldn't. And she would be disappointed in my silence.

"I'm not here for your sexual pleasure," I say, soft and slow. Barely believing that I'm saying anything. Hoping that maybe he doesn't hear me and leaves before the spirit of my penis-chopping great-grandmother completely possesses me.

Too late.

"What's that darling?" he asks.

I raise my voice. Loud and clear. "Every time you come in here, you make disgusting remarks about my body. About

Sandra's body. We don't like it. Stop it. Buy your buns here but shut the fuck up about our breasts and bums."

Everyone in the store goes quiet. Everyone is listening. Watching. Avidly. Even Sandra's gone quiet, her eyes wide open.

Kevin shifts uneasily, looks around and laughs a forced laugh. "Come on, it's a bit of fun. No harm done. Most women like some attention. Relax!"

I grip the cake knife tightly and channel the matriarch of Savaii as I brandish it in front of his face. "No. You listen and listen good because I'm only going to say this one time. It's not fun. Or funny. We don't want your nasty attention and the next time you reach across this counter and grab my breast? I will stick this knife through your hand. Like this." I stab the knife deep into the innocent cake, spearing it into the platter with a sharp thud.

Kevin's mouth gapes open, shocked and he jerks instinctively away from the counter. There's an ocean pounding in my chest and a cyclone crashing through my veins. Fear at war with courage.

The store erupts into applause as the line of customers cheer loudly. "You tell him girl!"

Kevin looks around once and then swivels and half-runs out of the store. Two women at the doorway hiss and boo at him as he races by.

I take a deep breath and try to calm my inner tempest.

"Right, " forced cheerfulness. "Who's next?"

In that moment, I think about the person that I try not to think about every day. Jackson. I want to call him, tell him what I've done. He would be so proud and happy for me. I clamp down hard on the thought and go about my work. Because Jackson is a door that I shut, a road I blocked off. The sooner I accept that and stop thinking about him, the better.

CHAPTER
Fourteen

wo weeks fly by and my job at the bakery comes to an end. It's official. I'm now a fulltime writer. My agent is excited. "You'll get so much more writing done now! Your publisher is rapt about getting more books from you. And your readers are hungry for more."

Her excitement should make me happy but it only makes me anxious.

That morning Nina notices and pauses before leaving for the office. "What's wrong? Your dream starts today doesn't it?" She fakes a drumroll and the roar of an imaginary crowd. "Aaaaannnnnnd let's hear it for the world famous New York Times bestselling author from Samoa, Nafanua Dane in the house!"

I have to smile, which is her intent. "I'm nervous. What if I can't do it?"

She puts her hands on her hips and gives me the raised eyebrow. "But you've already done it. You're not new to this game. You're not some newbie writer trying to break into the industry. You've written a romance series that's hit the USA Today and New York Times bestseller lists already. You have an agent who's out there selling you on three continents. And you have a Big Six publisher. You've already done it."

"No, Nafanua Dane's done all that. This will be my first time stepping out from behind the pen name. Writing as me. What if my readers don't like me?"

Another eye-roll. "Oh please. I think all your readers care about is getting to read more about Blade's magic cock. I know I want more of it. So get to work and give us some more books please!"

With that kind of encouragement, how can I possibly fail?

But before I open my laptop, there's one thing I need to do. It takes two trips but I'm determined, and within fifteen minutes of sweaty traipsing up and down the stairs, I've lugged all my father's books out to the trash. I don't hesitate or even indulge in a single twinge of guilty farewell before hurling the boxes into the dumpster. *There. It's done.* Now when I go back to the apartment, I feel light and free, a load lifted from my chest.

Naomi's right. I didn't need to be worried. For the next month, I bury myself in the writing. Words, paragraphs, chapters spill out onto the page in an almost desperate race to be unleashed. Like the past few years of writing in secret have been a dam of rigid control and now, there's nothing holding me back. My days are filled with stories, so many stories. I write about love, pain, heartache, joy, ecstasy, delight and struggle. I send pages to my agent and she raves about what she's calling the 'new direction' that my writing has taken. 'These are more real, raw and powerful!'

I shut myself away in my room and write some more, only emerging when hunger drives me out. Maybe its being away from the bakery, maybe it's the freedom from finally writing as myself, but food has become something secondary to me now. It's fuel, for my body. For my stories. Nina complains that she never sees me, bugs me to go out dancing with her and then leaves me alone when I tell her all I need is a few more weeks to get this writing madness out of me.

If my days are filled with stories, then my nights are filled with thoughts of Jackson. I hate it when the writing stops, when the stories hit the PAUSE button. Because then I can't keep the thoughts of Jackson at bay. I lie in bed and wonder where he is, what he's doing. Is he out on a date with some perfect corporate girlfriend? Maybe he's at the gym, doing a late night workout? Or is he in Texas visiting his family? I imagine what Elizabeth and Mark look like. His brothers. His family when they're all together. The house always has a white picket fence and there's an apple tree in the backyard. (Do apples even grow in Texas? I have no idea.) Jackson and his brothers sit around the table while their parents are at the opposite heads of the table. They eat roast steer and heaped bowls of cornbread. Elizabeth's made apple pie for dessert. With apples from the tree in the yard of course. Jackson and his brothers probably picked them and helped her in the kitchen.

Some nights thoughts of Jackson get me hot and bothered. I remember supply closets, plantations and sizzling hotel rooms. Then I have to get up and go take a cold shower. Which usually ends with me crying silent tears and softly slamming my clenched fist on the wall. I don't want Nina to know that I'm grieving. Or that I'm even thinking about Jackson. I'm doing a good job of pretending that I'm over him, that I don't care, that I've moved on, that I don't regret turning him down, that I'M NOT THINKING OF JACKSON AT ALL. EVER.

Some nights I torture myself by stalking his Facebook and Instagram. Which are sadly bereft of updates because Jackson is a man of few Facebook words. He hasn't posted anything new in over six months. I have to content myself with scrolling through his old tagged photos and posts. Honestly, why must the man be so damn reticent?! Why can't he be an over-sharer like the rest of us?

There's a lot of photos from two years ago. All posted by an ex-girlfriend called Francine Rogers. A petite ice blonde who barely comes up to his shoulder. She looks rich and there's lots of pics of them at fancy parties. Jackson wears a tux and he looks so delicious that I download some of the photos (and crop her out of course). A little voice in my head says that I'm indulging in behavior that can only be described as – stalker'ish. But I tell the voice to shut up. This is me grieving, I say, a necessary part of the process. Besides, doesn't everybody stalk their ex-lovers?

Jackson looks like he stepped out of a GQ magazine. Or he belongs at the Oscars. With a woman like Francine of course. I try with my very powerful imaginative powers, to insert myself into the pictures, into the gleaming dazzle of the fancy parties – but it's a dismal failure. No matter how hard I try, I can't see myself on his arm, smiling and chattering light chatter at the glittery events. Even in the most glorious evening gown that Nina has ever forced me into, I still cant imagine myself with Jackson, in *his* life. Just like I couldn't see him in my Samoa life either.

"See Scarlet?!" I mutter with damning intensity, "You did the right thing. There's no way you could have been Jackson's girlfriend. No fucking way. You would have been miserable and he would have ended up resenting you and dumping you. So there. You did him a favor. And saved yourself a bucket load of heartache. Be glad. You dodged a bullet."

So why am I so sad then? I bury my face in my pillow and cry some more.

I wonder – does he think of me at all? Does he miss me – ever? Probably not.

I thought I would be able to walk away from Jackson and not look back. I was wrong. Because the cold hard truth stabs me anew every night. I've fallen in love with him.

There's some benefits to the heartache though. The sadder and more lonely my nights are, the richer and more passionate my writing days become. I'm blogging too. Funny, fabulous, sarcastic and witty blogs about everything from my trip to Samoa, to my journey writing romance novels incognito as the daughter of a faifeau.

My agent Becca scores me the media opportunity of a lifetime. An interview feature piece with the New York Times. It makes me breathless just thinking about it and as soon as she tells me the news, I have an anxiety attack.

"What am I going to say?" I whine to Becca. "I can't do this!"

"Don't be silly. Of course you can," she snaps back. "I've sent you a list of questions she might ask so you can prepare because I know you like to be over-prepared for everything. But even if you didn't prep, you would rock this. Listen to me Scarlet. You're funny and brilliant and you've written some kickass books. Just imagine that you're talking to your blog readers and you'll be fine."

Becca is mean and pushy and everything that my agent should be, or else I would never leave my cave.

The interview goes well and I actually enjoy it. Becca sets up a session with a photographer for my author photo. Nina has a field day doing my hair and makeup. She makes me wear the scarlet wrap dress and I have a nervous attack of the giggles as I remember the wardrobe malfunction at Naomi's wedding.

"Make sure you keep your boobs in your dress during the photo shoot," cautions Nina with a cheeky grin.

I'm a nervous wreck waiting for the article to come out,

because what if I sound like a pathetic loser in my interview? But again, I needn't have worried. The write-up makes me sound funny and fabulous. (Totally not like me at all.) And sure I look like an orange pumpkin in the photo but Nina loyally pronounces me gorgeous and sensual, so I choose to focus on her words and allow myself to enjoy the thrill of being featured in the fucking New York Times baby! *Who me? Yes that's me!*

The day before the article comes out, my mother calls from Samoa. She makes no mention of our final conversation. Or any of the tortured details that we covered in that last gut-wrenching meeting. No, she prattles on like everything is still the same. Like we are still the same family we've always been.

For a few minutes I am angry, disappointed, stunned. I want to interrupt her, force her to confront the ugliness we last uncovered. But as she rattles on about Naomi, Tamarina, the babies, Father's newest book in progress, her church sewing group, Aunty Filomena...I know that I won't. Because this is the only way that my family knows how to be. This is the only way that my parents know how to love me. From a distance. With walls. With shuttered secrets safely bound in careful wrapping. And sure, I can refuse to accept that reality, and force them to remember and acknowledge the unspoken. Or I can go with it.

Do I need them to be what they aren't? Can I push forward without them?

Yes I can. Because this is my journey. Of healing and

survival. Peace and renewal. And I don't need them to take it with me.

So I listen to Mother and make the non-committal sounds that she needs to keep going. When there's gaps in the conversation I ask the questions that we are used to. About the children, and my sisters. About Aunty Filomena and can Mother please give her my love.

We finish the conversation as we always do. With Mother asking me about my weight, my eating, and whether I'm going to enroll at Stanford in the Master's program.

But today I do something different. I have news for her.

"I quit my job at the bakery."

Mother's gasp of shock gives me a buzz of pleasure. "E a? Really? So you're going back to school then!"

I let her dance along the path of assumption and happiness. Then I smash it to smithereens. Okay and maybe I take some pleasure in it. I'm only human. I'm not a fucking saint.

"No," I say. "I signed a publishing contract and I'm going to work fulltime as an author."

Mother is happy. Bubbling even. "Oh your father is going to be so proud. Walking in his footsteps."

Don't be too sure.

"I've actually been writing novels for two years now. Under a different name. My agent has been wanting me to go public so I can do promotional work for them and I finally agreed. So she's scored me a new three book deal with a big New York publishing company. Next month I'm doing my first book signing at the National Romance Writers Convention."

I can hear my mother's confusion and dread through the phone. I'm smiling to myself as I wait for her response.

"Romance? You write romance novels?"

"Yes. I have an erotic romance series and a sports romance series. My book deal is for my new plus size romance series. All the books have a gorgeous fat lead who finds love."

There's a long pause. "Erotic romance? I thought when you said you'd written a book, that you'd written a book like your father."

I laugh. "A religious theory book? Really Mother. I'm not a theologian."

"No, I mean a book that we could be proud of. Maybe an inspirational story. That we could put on the shelf and show to our friends and to everyone at church."

I'm cheerful and enjoying myself as I blaze ahead. "The covers aren't too trashy Mother, don't worry. I'll send you copies. You may not be able to display these in the church library but trust me, the women at church are going to love them. They'll bring some excitement to their lives. The first one in the new series is about a woman who works in a bakery. She's Samoan."

I can feel Mother's cold fear seeping through the connection. "You wrote about us? Your family? How can you do this to us?"

Right there is the crux of it. She's terrified that I will big mouth shout our family's secrets to the world. Break every Samoan rule on public face, shame, and reputation above all else. Expose us all.

"No Mother. The book isn't about our family. It's not about me either. Sure, there's some bits in there that are inspired by real experiences and real people, but that's what we writers do. We get inspiration from our life story and everyone in it, then we write fiction. Don't worry."

But she's not convinced. "You should have asked us first before you write these things and then let people read them!"

"You've been bugging me for years to stop wasting my potential and write something. You should be proud," I say without any apology. No fear. No shame. "My books are on the New York Times bestseller list. A Hollywood producer has optioned two of them for a movie. I was using a fake name before, but now I'm putting my real name on every book I write. Everyone will know it's me, your daughter!"

Then before she can fumble for an adequate response, I say goodbye and disconnect. Laughing. It feels good.

I'm singing to myself as I get back to work. I had thought for so long that it would be difficult to tell my parents that I write romance books, but now that I've done it? It feels great. Why didn't I do this sooner? Who cares if they don't like it?

As usual, I want to tell Jackson about my conversation with Mother, and my delighted relief to have the conversation done with. I allow myself a few minutes to imagine how that conversation would go. What I would say and how I would feel. The look in his eyes when I tell him.

I did it Jackson! I told my parents about my books. And the crazy thing? It wasn't hard at all. You were right. Thank you.

But I don't tell him. Because we aren't together. Because I broke up with him before we were even a couple. Because I asked him to leave me alone and give me space to sort out my shit. Because I'm an idiot.

I log on to Facebook again so I can stalk him. And again I'm disappointed because he still hasn't updated. *What the fuck is the point of having Facebook if you never post anything?!*

CHAPTER
Fifteen

BIG, BROWN AND BAREFOOT BLOG

I have an announcement. It's not earth-shattering, but it's something I've kept hidden for several years now and so it's a secret that's gotten more unnecessarily secret with each passing day.

I write romance novels under a pen name. Specifically, romance novels with lots of sex in them. The first few were self-published and then I got a publishing offer from a great New York company.

I was too scared to publish them under my real name so I used a made up one. Why was I scared? Lots of reasons that include privacy and the romance genre usually getting a bad rap. Because I have a degree in English Literature and my parents always wanted me to do a doctorate and be a Professor of English at some Very Important University and write Very Intellectually Profound books about Very Important and Intellectually Profound (Boring) things.

But the main reason would be, simply because I'm a Samoan woman.

For a long time, I worried what my extended family aiga

they would think of me if they knew I had written a sexy-time romance series. And everyone else.

I worried what my church would think. I worried what the woman at the bread shop would think, my second grade teacher, the policeman directing traffic, the bus driver who used to take us to school every morning, the man who hangs off the back of the rubbish truck and throws our bin every rubbish day and spills garbage all over the front of our house, the girls who called me meauli lapoa in 6th grade, and the list goes on…

The librarian who let me borrow ten books at a time when I was a teenager. I worried she would shake her head in disapproval and say, *'What a disappointment that girl is! She read so many books, she could have done something important and useful with her life. Instead of writing this trash!'*

The Sunday School teacher who smacked me with a ruler every time I got the words wrong in a scripture verse. She would nod knowingly and say, *"I knew it. She was always a wicked girl…"*

The English teacher who confiscated illicit Mills and Boon novels from me in class when I was twelve. She wouldn't be shocked at all. But she would purse her lips, push her glasses back and make a hacking spit sound of disgust at the back of her throat when she discussed it with everyone at my old school. *"She had unnatural tendencies from a young age. I tried to correct her, get it out of her. But it was impossible…"*

You get the idea right? Basically I was scared of what every single person I had ever known/seen/heard/ or even breathed the same air as would think if they found out.

But I have finally had a revelation. At the grand old age of thirty. (I'm a slow learner!) I have realised that

Most of the people I was worrying about – don't give a fuck about what I write, do, say, look like, or think. I need to get over myself!

And even if they did have an opinion, it doesn't matter.

Simple words but it's a massive weight rolled off my shoulders.

So this is me, Scarlet Thompson announcing to the world that I am the Big Brown Barefoot blogger. And I'm also 'Nafanua Dane', the author of the Sweet Passion series, the Red Card Rugby series and more. I'm pleased to meet you!

CHAPTER
Sixteen

*A*s I knew it would, any hope I had of keeping my books a secret from anyone in my family back home, is blown to smithereens by the New York Times article. The local newspaper picks up the story and Tamarina sends me a screenshot of my scarlet self on the front page of a stack of newspapers at the bread shop.

"The children said to tell you they're proud of their famous aunty. Tina wants to read them but I told her she has to wait till she's older. I'm proud of you too. Bought all your books on Amazon and started reading the first one last night. It's good. I couldn't stop reading till it finished. Jacob had to look after the twins. But your book inspired me and he got his reward so now he likes your book too."

Her message ends with winking and smiley face heart emojis. Somebody got busy last night!

Mother calls. I nearly don't answer. But then decide that it's best to rip the Band-Aid off quickly.

"Hi Mother. Another call so soon? Is everything alright?" Blasé innocence.

Her voice is a shaved ice cone when you bite down and

get that unpleasant stab of pain in your forehead. "Scar, did you have to wear that dress? The one that shows your susus to the whole world? Didn't you think of your poor Father and how this newspaper story would affect him? Or me your poor Mother? You could have worn your nice puletasi that I had made for you."

"Sorry Mother, I forgot that puletasi at the house. I left so suddenly you know?" Snarky hint at the dark things I know she doesn't want to talk about. It has the desired effect. Mother instantly backs off and there's no more talk of the indecency of my susus. Instead she switches to a much more important issue.

"So did you get paid by your publisher? We have a faalavelave coming up. Your cousin Malele is getting married and we have to put in a thousand tala."

Just like that we have smoothed over the tricky topic of my writing about S E X in trashy romance novels, as Mother takes refuge in the safety of the familiarity of faalavelave.

I promise to send some money and hang up with a combination eye roll and hi-five, glad for the millionth time that Mother can't see me through the internet. Who said money can't give you happiness? If you're Samoan, then money solves many problems and bridges all divides. Why didn't I figure it out sooner? As long as I keep making my contributions to the family, then it seems my parents can endure anything of me.

Beyonce calls to congratulate me, to shower me with

praise and love. "I knew it girl! I always knew you would be rich and famous one day!"

"I'm not rich and I'm not famous either. The highest my books have ever hit on the list was 12th. That doesn't get me on any famous lists!"

"That makes you famous on my list," counters my cousin. "So have you tracked down Jackson yet?"

It doesn't matter how many times I tell Beyonce that I've broken everything off with Jackson, and all the reasons why – she refuses to accept it. "Don't be stupid. He doesn't care about any of that stuff. Besides, why should he have to suffer because of your family dramas? Call him. Tell him you're sorry and you want to make it up to him. In lots of sexual ways."

Beyonce made it sound easy. Possible. Doable. I didn't share her positivity. Because when a man like Jackson offers you the world, and you politely say *no thanks*? The world doesn't give you a second chance at that. The fact that I even got a first chance at that is crazy ridiculous in and of itself.

With every passing day though, I am kicking myself more as I second-guess my breakup with Jackson. It seemed like the right thing to do at the time. The noble, morally upstanding thing to do. The choice that heroes in artsy Oscar-winning movies make all the time, where she walks away from her one true love because she's too damaged to love the way he deserves...or because she has to sacrifice herself and save the world instead…or because she knows he would be happier and better off with someone else. And then everybody dies tragically.

Fuck I hate those movies. They suck.

My Aunties Amalia and Mareta are loving my news. They insist I give them an entire signed set of all my books and then invite me and Nina over for Sunday lunch so they can proudly show off their shelf display.

We walk into the living room and stop still and shocked at the sight. The Jesus portraits are no longer the main feature. The Aunties have framed the New York Times article and now my scarlet-wrapped susus are forever immortalized on their wall. And my books! Each book is on its very own little easel stand with plastic flower leis draped in between so that the collection takes up an entire shelf on the main wall. It means the covers are on full display. Blade's rippling muscles and glistening chiseled torso leap out at you the minute you walk in and its impossible to miss Farah's heaving bosom and luscious curves busting out of her baker's apron as she kisses him enthusiastically. I don't think I ever noticed before how big Westley's hands are as they grip a rugby ball, holding it in a strategic position in front of his naked tattooed self. *Oh my…* My books have turned the Aunties living room into a showcase of steamy allure.

The Aunts stand there smiling proudly as they wait for our reaction.

"You like?" asks Amalia eagerly.

"Wow," says Nina, walking forward with her hands outstretched. "Like? I love! Isn't it beautiful Scarlet?"

I have no words. I'm torn between cringing and laugh-crying.

"It's so lovely to see how proud you are of Scarlet's work," continues Nina, giving me a sharp nudge. "The silly girl had been worried that you wouldn't be happy about her writing."

Amalia and Mareta exchange bemused looks. "Not happy? But why?"

Aunty Mareta goes to straighten the framed news article. "Scarlet, you're in the newspaper! You make our family famous and bring us so much pride." She looks near-tearful as she beams at me. "We so happy for you. Malo lava."

'Y'hear that Scarlet? They're so HAPPY for you." Nina nudges me again. I'm getting bruises from all the #IToldYouSo poking that I'm getting here.

Amalia frowns, "Yes, but I don't know why you kept it a secret from us for so long? We worried about you staying at the bakery forever when we know you got a talent from God for writing. The Bible says, don't hide your talents Scarlet."

Mareta jumps in. "Yes. You must use your talents to bring honor to your family. And bring joy to others. I'm thinking these books are making many people feel happiness."

Nina arches an eyebrow. "Oh ah know they do! Have you read any of them yet Aunty? No? Can I suggest you begin with the first book in the Red Card rugby series? It's called ADVANTAGE. There's a few scenes in there that I think will bring you quite a bit of happiness…" The three women move to the kitchen, as Nina continues telling the aunties about how deliciously happy the books make her.

I should be horrified that Nina's recommending my elderly aunty read the most erotic out of all my books, and that Mareta is nodding earnestly. I should tell Nina to shush. But I can't because I'm trying not to cry. My aunts are proud of me. Happy that I have brought honor and recognition to our family. They're glad I'm using my talents to write romance novels. Their living room wall is practically a shrine to their pride in me, their celebration of me.

It's beautiful. And so very humbling.

In that moment I am dreadfully ashamed. Why didn't I have more faith in them? They had always treated me with love and kindness, and taken me in as their own, treated me like their daughter. Why did I think that they would condemn me for my books? Why was I so determined to believe the worst of everyone who loved me?

It seemed that some of the walls I'd been trapped behind for so long, so much of my worry and fear – had been of my own making. Elaborately constructed inside my own imaginings. The lighted path had always been there, but I had chosen to see only the mists of darkness.

The truth is - we can't leave Pulotu until we are ready.

I sit at the table with a smile frozen on my face as Aunty Amalia dishes me up huge servings of faalifu kalo and chop suey, as Aunty Mareta announces they got pisupo because it's a 'day for celebrating!' I listen as the Aunties ask Nina about her boyfriend, and then make sympathetic noises as she tells them about her breakup.

Mareta leans across the table to pat Nina's hand soothingly. "He was not good enough for you. Be patient. The right one will come one day. But make sure you're not distracted by a trash man in case you miss the right one."

"It's not easy to find the right person," adds Amalia sagely. "But when you do, you don't let them go."

Nina jumps in, "Did you hear that Scarlet? When you find the right person, you don't let them go."

I ignore her teasing and instead I get up and go to hug first Amalia and then Mareta. Emotion catches in my throat and words are difficult but I try anyway. Just because we are staunch Samoans, doesn't mean we can't change. Adapt. Bend. Soften. And love each other out loud. "Thank you Aunty. For always loving me and taking such good care of me. For being proud and encouraging of me. I love you both so much."

They are surprised, but pleased. "Teine lelei. Good girl," they say and there is so much love and unity in the room that we nearly forget about the caramel coconut puligi that Aunty Mareta made for dessert.

CHAPTER
Seventeen

JACKSON

*T*he buzzer on my desk goes and I swear. Can't I ever get a single minute of peace around here? What's the point of being the CEO of the company if nobody listens to anything you say? I ignore it but it buzzes again.

"What is it Rex?" I snap.

Rex is apologetic. "You have a visitor Mr. Emory."

"I said no visitors. Tell them to fuck off." I disconnect before he can say anything more and stride over to the window. It's an incredible view looking out over the expanse of city, but I don't see it. Instead I see a lush green rainforest thousands of miles away, and a woman laughing at me with her arms full of ruby red flowers. A woman who walked out of my life without looking back. Leaving me a note.

Again the buzzer goes and I lose it. Pick up the machine, yank the wire out and throw it across the room where it smashes against the wall. The rage is building. It's been simmering for a while now, but it's getting to break point.

I hear the door open behind me

"I'm sorry Mr. Emory. I tried but..." says a hesitant Rex.

I turn, ready to curse him out, but stop when I see who's standing beside him in the doorway.

"Elizabeth?"

"It's not his fault. He did try to tell me to *fuck off*' but I wouldn't take no for an answer," she says with a smile as she pats my subdued assistant on the shoulder. "Thank you Rex." He nods, avoiding my gaze, and scurries away. Relieved to be escaping no doubt.

My second mother strolls in and sits at my chair. Which used to be her chair. She kicks off her heels, leans back and puts her feet up on my desk. "I like what you've done with the place."

"I haven't changed anything since you were here last month."

She shrugs and stares pointedly at the heap of metal and wire in the corner. "Oh really?"

"An engineering malfunction," I say.

"You should know. Since you're the engineer," she says. "But it looks more like a temper tantrum to me."

"What are you doing here?" I ask again.

"Oh, I was in the neighborhood. Thought I would stop by and see my favorite son."

In the neighborhood? Stop by? - It's a three hour direct flight from Houston to Vegas, and we both know it. I grit my teeth and fight to calm the turmoil within. Walk over to give her a hug. I'm only doing it because it's what I'm supposed to do, but when she holds me close, I feel some of my tension ease. She lets me go but not without first whispering, "It's good to see you son."

Since she has my desk, I sit on the couch and brace myself for whatever has brought Elizabeth to my office. She gets straight to the point with her characteristic incisiveness.

"What's happened?"

I deflect. "What do you mean? All our projects are on target. We just scored another building over in the East district."

She says nothing. She simply waits. It's a trick she used on us all the time when we were kids. Sit there and say nothing, let us squirm, and then one of us would end up cracking and blurting out answers to questions she never even asked. I often use it now in negotiations and I am not going to let her use it on me.

"So you're not here to talk about business."

"Of course not," she says. "This isn't my company any more. I'm retired, remember?"

"Why don't you save us both some time then and ask what you came here to ask?" I counter.

"How was your trip to Samoa?" she asks.

'Fine," I say. "Did you see the wedding photos I sent to the family chat?"

She smiles. "They were beautiful. Troy looks so happy. And such interesting wedding customs. I'm proud of you helping that woman give birth safely. It's so beautifully sweet that now there's a little baby named after you all the way on a distant tropical island! I told Mark we should take our next holiday in Samoa. Maybe we can finally wrangle all you boys to do that family vacation I've been wanting for ages now. With enough advance warning, surely you can all get your schedules aligned so you can go on vacation with your aged ailing parents?"

Elizabeth and Mark are in their early sixties and the perfect picture of health, but still her choice of words has me worried. "Are you two okay? You haven't come to tell me you're sick?"

Her face softens at the concern in my voice. She comes over to sit beside me on the couch. "No. I'm fine. And so is Mark. He was on the roof this morning repairing the guttering. Right after we went for our ten mile run. We have our marathon next weekend remember?"

Since Elizabeth stepped down as CEO of Emory Steel three years ago, she had thrown herself into retirement with the same intensity she had brought to the company. Mark would have been happy with his horses and playing cards with the usual crowd every Friday night, but Elizabeth had roped him into taking up running with her. Now they were adventure tourists, travelling the world to run in different events, and forever trying to persuade their sons to go with them.

"I promise you, I'm not here because Mark or I are sick. I'm sorry if I gave you that impression," says Elizabeth. She reaches over and hugs me again, and for a moment I am a teenager. In a hospital, watching my birth mother die of cancer, with Elizabeth and Mark there to support me through it.

"No, I'm here because while I may be retired from this company, I will never retire from being your mother and from worrying about you," says Elizabeth firmly. "Now you know I wouldn't interfere in your life, you're a grown man now."

I have to smile at that because Elizabeth wouldn't be Elizabeth if she didn't 'interfere' in my life and my crazy brothers lives. She sees my grin and knows why. Gives me a prim sniff and continues.

"But when I get calls from your brothers, worried about you – then I have to respond. What kind of mother would I be if I didn't?"

Screw those idiots. What have they been telling her?

"Look Mom, I don't know what the guys have told you, but I'm fine," I assure her.

"You haven't been going to Saturday basketball with them," she accuses me.

"I've been busy working on a quote. I had to miss a few weekend games. Big deal!"

"Matilda says she hasn't seen you or heard from you in over a month," adds Elizabeth, her eyes flashing with determined fire as she builds her case for my not being okay. "She's your best friend. Why wouldn't you be talking to her?"

"Mom, Matilda just had a baby. I'm giving her and Theo some space with their new daughter. It's not a sign that I'm falling apart. It's your son being considerate and thoughtful."

Elizabeth takes a deep breath and says in a quiet tone of finality. "You crashed your Ferrari. And you didn't tell us."

There it is. The biggest missile warning in her arsenal. I don't even want to know how she found that out. It wouldn't surprise me at all if she had contacts at every mechanic shop in the state.

"What's going on Jackson? Are you racing again?" And the unspoken question is stamped in the air between us. *Are you fighting again?* She reaches across and takes my hand in hers. "You can tell me. Mark and I, we only want to help. But you have to tell us what's going on."

The long-ago kid I used to be would get angry right now. Push her hand away. Get defensive aggressive. Yell. Storm out. Look for someone to beat the shit out of.

Elizabeth knows this, and still she is here, asking, searching, worrying. My adoptive parents have been through a lot with me. My acting out, rebellious stage had lasted a little longer than most teenagers and included an addiction to the high of illegal drag racing and the thrill of fight clubs. It's been ten years since they last had to extricate me from a mess of my own making, but I accept that this visit is a sign they care. Not of a lack of trust.

"I wasn't drag racing. And I'm not back in the ring again. I promise. But I *was* speeding that night. Took a corner too fast and spun out," I explain.

"Were you hurt? Was anyone else hurt?" she asks.

"No." Then I go for total disclosure. Because she's my mother and she's flown all the way here to check up on me. "I did give the cops some hassles though when they responded to the accident. I had to go in to the station. They pulled up my record."

She doesn't like that. "Oh Jackson, you should have called us."

"What for? It was late. I sorted it out. Got my lawyer. Everything's been dealt with." Give her a reassuring smile. Squeeze her hand. Project reassurance, calmness and general 'Your son is a mature adult who has everything under control...'

She's not convinced. "Why were you speeding anyway? Remember what the therapist said about pushing limits and crossing boundaries? Warning signs?"

I concede. "I've had some things on my mind. That I need to figure out. Personal things."

She's visibly glad that I'm letting her in. Even that little bit. "Have you talked to someone about it?" she asks. By 'someone' she means a therapist.

"No. I'm dealing with it," I say. Brusque, because I don't want her to push any further than she already has.

"Alright. But son, that there?" She points at the debris that used to be the intercom machine. "The cursing out of your PA? That's not you. Not you at your best anyway." She stands. "I'm going to get out of your way. I promised Mark I would get back in time for a late supper. I wanted to see you, and tell you in person that we love you and miss you. Come down to the ranch soon for a visit, okay? Please?"

I assure her I will. I'm touched she's come all this way to check on me and now has another flight to take back home. All in one day. "I love you Mom. Tell Dad I miss him."

But Elizabeth isn't done. She is almost to the door when she pauses, turns back. That calculating look in her eyes is one I've seen many times when she was in CEO mode. "You extended your stay in Samoa. Why?"

"Umm, what do you mean?" Immediately I mentally kick myself. *Wrong move.* By trying to sidestep her, I have put a screaming siren on this path of questioning.

"You were only supposed to be gone a week. But you stayed longer. Why?" She's looking around the office now as if some clue to the puzzle might be somewhere in plain sight. She's talking softly, almost to herself. "You're not sleeping, you're speeding, bursts of rage, you didn't shave this morning or yesterday either by the looks of it, you won a big contract worth twenty million but you're not happy, work isn't giving you what it used to…" She spins around to face me again. "You met someone there."

It's a pronouncement, not a question. There's not much point my refuting it. This is Elizabeth Emory after all.

I shrug. Tired. Defeated. *You got me.* "But I don't want to talk about," I say.

She doesn't fight me on it. Instead she comes to hug me tight. "Oh son, you don't have to." She steps back, looks up at me, astute observation. "She means a lot to you. I can tell. But I'm not going to pry. You'll tell us when you're ready. I'll be waiting to hear from you. But Jackson, I didn't raise you to sit around and mope. To fester like this. I taught you to act. If something – or someone – is this important to you? Then you get out there and you fix whatever's wrong. You do your best, you go all out and you do what you have to do."

With that final reminder, she blows me a kiss and exits.

CHAPTER
Eighteen

SCARLET

The invite comes to my inbox. Along with plane tickets. Richard's exhibit is opening in Los Angeles. It's called **FIERCE**. I click on the attachment. It's a flyer for the show. There's a black and white image of a woman. She laughs into the camera, head thrown back, arms crossed. A dusting of sand on gleaming wet skin. Bold thighs and lush curves. It's titled JOY.

She is magnificent. Unafraid. Unapologetic. She's wholly and truly alive, and issuing you with the bold invitation to rejoice with her and in her.

She is beautiful.

She is me.

I hate Los Angeles. The airport alone is enough to have you wishing you were somewhere else. Anywhere else. I get a cab straight to the gallery. I'm only here for the day. I don't want to be in this city for any longer than I need to be. I've purposely chosen to come in the middle of the day because I want to slink in unnoticed, take a furtive glimpse of my picture on the wall and then get the hell out of here. After taking a photo of course. I need visual evidence that I was once a cover model.

But there's a crowd at the doors. Not moving, just standing. "What's going on?" I ask a random woman in the line. "Something happened to the show?"

She gives me a funny look. "This is the line. We're waiting to go in."

Seeing my puzzlement, she says, "Haven't you been to a Richard Brandt show before?"

"No. This is my first," I confess.

"They're always packed out," she explains.

"But it's been open since Monday?"

She responds with disbelief at my ignorance, a generous serving of art snobbery. "It's Richard Brandt. Every piece sold by the end of the first day."

Oh. I don't know whether to be hyped that someone has bought my picture – or sad because it means there's no hope I can buy it (for a much much discounted pity price) when nobody wants it.

Finally it's our turn to get inside the doors. There's

another crush of people waiting in the outer reception area. A group exits in a rush of expensive perfume. A man in a red suit bumps into me. He mumbles an automatic apology. But then he looks at me and there's a flash of something – recognition? "It's you," he says. Surprise and something else. Something admiring. He turns to his friends. "It's her!"

Then there's a surreal moment. A flurry of exclamations, handshakes, congratulations and compliments. 'Beautiful... stunning...so much celebration...exquisite...perfect model...Brandt's truly outdone himself this time...'

Flustered and bemused, I smile inanely, shake hands and smile some more. I have no idea what they're talking about. I'm only grateful that I wore the green wrap dress and let Nina do nice things to my hair. Otherwise nobody would be able to connect me with Richard's picture.

"Thank you," I say. I think. "I'm glad you liked it."

"I loved all of them," the red suit man says expansively.

All of them? What's he talking about?

Then I step inside and I know.

On one side of the room, are three giant canvases that take up the entire wall, floor to ceiling. Of me. Down another wall are five more. Of me. In the next overflow room is a wall with five more pictures. Of me. On the beach. In the water. Sitting on the sand with the white lace of foam around me. Leaning against patterned lava rock and looking out to the horizon. He even captured that frenzied moment when the wave smashed into me – the exhilarated surprise on my face, my arms outreached to the sky with the deluge of water frozen all around me.

It's all there. On full display for everyone and their dog to look at. My legs, just skimmed by the scrap of wet lava-lava tied low on my hips. Taro thighs and rugby-player calves. My breasts – covered thank goodness – but practically spilling out of the halter top. My belly, *awww fuck*, there it is, the generous swell and curve. No Spanx. No sucking in. No carefully angled camera shot. Just me. All of me.

I can't breathe. I want to run and hide but I'm rooted to the spot. Panic chokes me. Shame paralyzes me. I want to cry. How could he do this to me? How could he put me on display like this? I feel ill.

There's a press of people behind me so I can't back out of there. A stand of greenery calls to me from a corner. Temporary sanctuary. I go to it, head down, and then stand there trying to stop the shaking. *Deep breaths. You can do this. Don't fall apart.*

But as I stand there, the murmuring of the crowd ebbs and flows around me. Snatches of conversation. Some discussing the photography with technical words I don't understand, and others remarking on the model. On me.

"Stunning."

"The   symmetry…the   lushness…joyous…wild…

freedom...unashamed...happy...so beautiful...natural..."

Slowly, the shame and panic subsides and in their place is something else. A surprised kind of awe.

They like the pictures. I remember that day. Richard's directives and reassuring words. But more than that, I remember Jackson. Coaxing a smile from me, putting me at ease, transforming that afternoon from something painful to something lighthearted and fun.

Of course. It made perfect sense now. *Joy.*

Then I walk around the corner and there he is. The broad arms, the strong sure lines of his torso, the dancing light in his eyes as he laughs down at me with his hair clinging to his forehead. I come to a standstill. All the pictures in the exhibit are of me alone. Except for these three. Richard has captured three perfect shots of me. And Jackson.

One of us from a distance, while we're sitting in the shade. We aren't looking at the camera, totally unaware of it's presence. I must be talking because I've got my hands up, one of my crazy hand motions forever caught on camera while I blather on about something intense. Jackson is looking at me. Even in the removed profile, the expression on his face is unmistakable. He looks like a man entranced. By every ridiculous word coming out of my mouth. Which can't possibly make sense.

Can it?

The second print is of us in the water. He's pulled me up out of the churning foam and I'm a drenched mess with my shirt clinging to everything I don't want it to. He has his arms around me and I'm leaning back against his chest – laughing. Looking straight at the camera, utterly delighted and alive. And who wouldn't be? With all that glorious man pressed against you, I ask? We look happy. Together. We look like we belong. Together. Which makes no sense.

Does it?

But it's the final picture which knocks the air out of me. Richard must have taken it right after Jackson tripped and fell in the shallows, with me in his arms. I'm lying on the sand, with Jackson above me, sinewy arms on either side as he holds himself poised above me. Neither of us is smiling. Because we're staring into each other's eyes, oblivious to the world around us. Because we are well and truly lost in each other, like it's the most perfect thing to be lying on itchy sand on a beach in the middle of the Pacific Ocean. We look like we're in love. Which makes no sense. At all.

Right?

In the cab, through the ugly bleakness of LAX and all the long way home, I am quiet. Thinking of a slideshow of black and white images going through my mind. Yes I'm excited to be the star of a Richard Brandt exhibit and proud that every single photo has sold, but more than that – I'm sad. Unbearably so. Because seeing Jackson and I together in blown-up proportions has confirmed what I've been mulling over in the back of my mind since I left Samoa.

I was wrong to say no to him. To break up before we even began. To shut down the possibility of us. Why didn't I just tell him what had happened in my confrontation with my mother? Tell him I was sad, confused, and needed a bit of time to process it all? Why couldn't I have trusted that he would be capable of handling a few more of my secrets? Why couldn't I see then that what we had, would have been strong enough to bridge the messy differences between us? Sure it would have been a crazy leap of faith, but whatever happened, wherever that wild dance took us – it would have been worth it. He was worth it.

I'm ready now. To take that leap. But Jackson's gone. And no amount of cake is going to bring him back.

At home I debrief with Nina over sundaes. I come unglued. Completely. Crying into my melting chocolate.

"You said you didn't care any more. You said you were over him," accused Nina.

"I lied," I sob into my ice cream. "I miss him so much. Every day. I think about him. Every night. I didn't think I was worth him. I didn't believe we had a chance."

"And now?"

"Now I know I was wrong. But its too late!" I hiccup

and blow my nose on the tablecloth.

Nina gives me a look of disgust. 'Ugh. That's not true. You can call him." She hands me the phone. "Right now."

"And what?" I splutter, terrified at the very thought of Jackson's voice on the phone.

"Tell him you're sorry. You made a mistake. Tell him how you feel."

"I can't," I say, horrified.

"Why not?" she demands.

"Because there's no way he's still single. Or even thinking about me. It's been months since Samoa. Months! He's long over me. And he's got hordes of willing women in his bed by now. Like revolving doors of them! If I call him, then he'll know how I feel about him. There will be a beautiful woman waiting for him in his bed, naked – while I'm pouring out my heart on the phone."

"What would be so wrong about that?" shrugs Nina. "Love is risky. Scary. It means getting vulnerable. Letting people in to hurt you. Sure he might turn you down. But he might not. Isn't your happiness worth taking that risk? And besides, it hasn't even been that long."

I decide that Nina was right. But I don't call Jackson. Instead, I write him a letter. One that the whole world can read. Because the new Scarlet Thompson can't just do things quietly and on the down-low. No. The best way to show Jackson that I'm ready to stop hiding my feelings for him, is to do as he asked me. *Go public. Say yes to him.* Because romance this big requires - going big or going home.

CHAPTER
Nineteen

BIG, BROWN AND BAREFOOT BLOG

A Love Letter

I met a man on a plane. He was #NotJasonMomoa. He made me laugh. He made me feel safe. With him, I was someone else. Someone funny, strong, assured and beautiful. Someone that gorgeous strangers on airplanes would want to hook up with. When I thought we would crash and die, he held my hand and said, "Don't worry. I'm here. I won't let go." I believed him. And the possibility of descending to earth in a fiery ball of carnage, no longer frightened me.

I danced with a man at a birthday party. He was #NotJasonMomoa. Together, we were every cheesy dancing couple in every dancing romance movie. Flashdance. Grease. Saturday Night Fever. High School Musical. Even Step Up, parts One, Two and Three. He held me in his arms and said, "What are you afraid of? Why don't you want anyone to see the real you?" I had no answer. Not then anyway. So we just danced and it was perfection.

I fell over onto a man at the beach. Squished the air right out of him. He was #NotJasonMomoa. He rescued me from a surprise wave. Lifted me up out of a washing machine spin of sand and saltwater and then I had to go and fall on him. Of course. We laughed. Being there in his arms, under a wild grey sky was right. It's where I was meant to be. He said, "You're beautiful." I laughed. When what I should have said was, Thank You. When what I should have said was, So are you.

I looked at stars with a man in Samoa. A scattering of black diamonds on a velvet expanse of sky. He was #NotJasonMomoa. He talked of apple pie and the bones of my spine, the bite of my teeth. He said, "We are hewn of stars, and only when I look at you, do I believe it." And he didn't laugh afterwards. Imagine that! It wasn't a joke. He actually meant it. In that moment, I felt as brilliant and as eternal as those distant stars, light years of being.

I loved a man in a rainforest as the full-bellied sky burst with heaviness. He was #NotJasonMomoa. Warm rain and the crush of teuila all overlaid with the heady fragrance of ripe mosooi wilting in the noonday sun. He promised the only thing I would be drunk on – was him. And he spoke true.

I couldn't look as a man delivered a baby in the backseat of a car. He was #NotJasonMomoa. He soothed with calm words and guided with strong sure hands. He stilled my frantic panic and together we watched as they delivered the second of my sister's twins. Tears, sweat and blood coalesced into two perfect tiny humans. Then tired and bloodstained, he smiled at me. In his smile I saw the possibility of a future together.

He was not Jason Momoa.

He was something so much better. He was real and flawed and complicated. He saw through my lies and didn't run from my secrets. I was afraid and I sent him away. I messed up.

If you're reading this, if you even still think of me, then know that I'm sorry.

Please come back.

CHAPTER
Twenty

hen my publisher had suggested they sign me up to be a featured author at the annual Romance Readers Convention, I almost said *hell no*. Who would come to my table? I'd be the only fool sitting there without a single person wanting my signature while all around me, the REAL authors were fighting off the adoring fans. No was on the tip of my tongue. But then I remembered a quizzical smile and the raised eyebrow, *'Why are you so afraid for people to see the real you?'* I heard my great-aunt say, *'You are too much living afraid.'* So I gave myself a kick in the backside, figuratively speaking of course, and said yes.

A decision I'm still second-guessing, right up until I walk into the convention hall and see the line waiting at my table.

"That can't be right," I mutter to Becca. "Must be the wrong table."

She laughs. "It's got your name on it."

There it is. A big bold placard reads,

SCARLET THOMSON
Writing as NAFANUA DANE

There's even a banner with the same words, suspended over the table and as Becca walks me up to the table, there's an excited buzz from the waiting crowd. "It's her," someone says.

"Hi Ms. Dane!" another calls out. "I love your books."

I sit down and grip the table edge tightly to stop my hands from shaking. Becca gives me a reassuring pat on the shoulder. "You'll be fine," she whispers. "Just be yourself and have fun."

I look up at the league of excited faces, countless strangers who have read my stories and devoured my words and I feel faint. How can I possibly have fun? These people have been party to my innermost thoughts and fancies. They've poured over every one of my words – even the sexy bits. *Oh hell, especially the sexy bits.* How could they not think I'm a complete whore?

Stop it Scar! That's the shamed and shameful woman inside you talking there. Shut up.

"You ready?" asks Becca.

I nod, not trusting my voice.

"Right. This is how it works," she explains. "To move it along, there's a limit of three books per person and everyone's had to write the names on a Post-it of who they want the books signed to. That way you don't have to waste time asking for spelling. We're allowing pictures but only while you're signing their books and I have Jonas and Alex here who will help take the photos using their phone camera. No-one is to touch you or come to your side of the table. The boys will make sure you're okay all throughout."

Jonas and Alex are two nice looking men in jeans and suit jackets. They give me reassuring smiles and I feel marginally better. I'm not worried about anybody invading my personal space or going into a fangirl fit – because let's face it, its far more likely that I'll have a meltdown and hide under the table, rocking on my knees. But having them as backup crew is like having a team of supporters guaranteed to be on my side. If only because they're getting paid to be.

"Right. You ready?" asks Becca. Again.

"Yes. Bring it on." *Ha, that sounded strong and confident! Let's do this.*

I plaster a smile on my face and the first person runs over to perch on the seat in front of the table. A tiny young woman, in her twenties maybe? She's clutching an armful of books to her chest like they're precious cargo. Like she's worried somebody's going to jump her any minute and steal them.

"Ohmagosh, ahm sooo exsaahhted! Ahh cant believe aaahm meetin ya!" she gushes so effusively that I have trouble deciphering her rich southern accent. A hand over her heart as she takes on a soulful expression. "Bryant is the most amaaahzin man ahh have evah met. Ahh just love him." Bryant being the love interest in one of my Red Card romance series books.

"Why thank you," I say. "I'm quite partial to him myself."

She chatters on about all Bryant's redeeming qualities as she hands me her precious books with a Post-it stuck on top and right then I want to cry. I want to freeze this moment, right here, right now and remember it forever. My first real fan. My first ever-signing. My first ever moment where I feel like a real live author. I sign her books and try not to drip tears on the pages. It takes everything I have not to leap up and hug her, not to sob loudly, *Oh thank you for reading my books!'*

Then it's the next person's turn, this time an older woman with greying hair in a bun. She tells me the books are for her grand-daughter who couldn't get off work to come to the signing. "She adores your work," she says. "She's read all your books at least six times over. Worships Bryant." Then, just before she gets up to go, she leans forward to whisper conspiratorially, "But I'm a Harrison fan myself. Bad-boys do something wicked to me, y'know?"

And so it goes. Everyone is friendly and full of encouragement and praise. For the characters. For the love scenes. For the romance. For the honeymoons in the Pacific islands especially. For convincing bad boys. I'm not freaking out anymore because I'm having the time of my life. Who knew that there were this many people in the world who actually read my books? And liked them enough to stand in line to meet the author and get her signature? I sure didn't.

Two hours go by and my hand's getting sore. My cheeks are hurting from all the smiling. I'm shifting into automaton mode. *Hi, lovely to meet you! What name do you want your books signed to? Thank you so much for your book support. I'm so glad you enjoyed them. Yes, the next book will be out soon….Hi, lovely to meet you! What name do you want your books signed to?…blah blah.*

Becca comes over to let me know I can take a break in another ten minutes. *Thank goodness.* I need a burger. Fries. A milkshake. And an apple pie. Possibly two.

I say goodbye to the bubbly teenager who I suspect is nowhere near old enough to be reading about Bryant's throbbing manhood and then reach for the next book on the table as another person steps forward. Without looking up, I get the Post-it stuck on top of the cover. "Hi, lovely to meet you. What name do you want your book signed to?"

A glance at the writing on the yellow slip of paper.

#NotJasonMomoa

Time stops. Everything comes to a crashing halt. *It can't be…*

I look up.

It is.

Jackson is standing in front of me with the hint of an enigmatic grin. I drink him in hungrily. Two months is not that long but it seems like a millennium. He is an oasis in the midst of a wasteland and I drink him in hungrily. The crinkled edges of his dark eyes. The lock of hair hanging over his right eye. The line of his jaw with its rough edge of bristle. His mouth – which makes me immediately think of all the things he can do with it. The sheer size of him as he towers over me in a suit jacket over an open-necked shirt. He radiates sensuality and I am drowning in it.

Breathe Scar.

From far away, I think he says something. But I cant make it out through my dazed haze so he has to lean forward and repeat it.

"I got your message," he says, and the grated coconut edge of his voice is a delicious treat.

"My message?" I say inanely. Then it makes sense. "Oh." Comprehension dawns. "You read my blog." I stand up so abruptly that my chair falls over backward. The crash resounds through the hall and Alex races to pick it up. Everybody's looking now. Suddenly I'm regretting my very public love letter appeal. Because now he is here, in this very public place. *What was I thinking?!*

I shut my eyes for a moment and wish for this to be a dream. But when I open them again, he's still there. I want him to go away. But I also never want him to leave. A rush of wanting hits me, so powerful so overwhelming that I almost fall over.

"What are you doing here?" I ask. When really, I want to tell him how breathlessly happy I am to see him. Be this close to him.

"To get my book signed of course. Plus, I brought you something."

He hands me a cake box. I open it. Cookies. A little misshapen and crumbly, but most certainly cookies. White chocolate chip and macadamia nut.

"I made them," he offers. "From your recipe on the blog."

Little pitter-patter footprints of joy dance through me. "You made me cookies?"

He is delightfully rueful. "Still haven't got 'em right. I've been practicing. This is my fourth try. You never told me baking was dangerous." He holds out his hand. "Burnt it trying to get them out of the oven." In that moment, I can imagine him in the kitchen, sweaty and harassed, trying to make my favorite cookies, getting frustrated.

I take his hand, loving the feel of it in mine, pretending to study it. He's telling the truth. There's a raised red blister burn on two fingers. I can't resist. I blow softly on the burn and then kiss his palm. That's when the watching crowd erupts. Cheers and catcalling. But I don't hear them. Me and Jackson are now in our own perfect bubble of white chocolate macadamia cookies, sweetly rich with so many unspoken words and unwrought emotion. I raise my eyes to his. "That's so sweet of you," I say inanely, "I can't believe you did that for me."

A shrug. "Trying to check everything on the list."

"Huh? What list?"

He counts off on his fingers. "The list for Scarlet's perfect boyfriend. One, must have big muscles – which I think we've established already can certainly carry you."

Oh we sure did. Fire flames at my face at the memory. But he's not done. "Two, not be ugly. Your nieces assure me I pass that measure. Three, should be fun and funny." A fake frown. "I'm nowhere near as funny as you but I'm trying. And four, can I make cookies. That, I'm working on." He continues, hesitant now. "I was thinking, maybe when you're done here – we could go get a coffee. Talk. You could try the cookies. Give me some tips."

"Yes. I want you – I mean I want to."

He laughs and everything is right with us. He's holding my hand across the table and it feels right. The universe realigns and everything is in synch again. Jackson is here.

I rush on, "It's my break now."

Taking my cue, Becca steps in with a smile and a pleasant but firm announcement for the remaining readers. Something about Scarlet going for a thirty minute lunch break and she'll be back soon. But I'm not listening because Jackson has tugged me around the table and into his arms so he can kiss me. Again the crowd of readers is cheering. Phone cameras are flashing.

It's a long, slow kiss of re-acquaintance, delicately tasting and teasing. He is the milky sweetness of white chocolate and the salt tang of macadamia. I come up for air and say, "You ate some of my cookies!"

He grins. "I had to taste them didn't I? Chef's privileges."

From far away I am conscious of the curious eyes and the hushed buzz of onlookers, the amused questioning stares of my team. I tip-toe to whisper in his ear. "Let's get out of here."

He takes my hand in his as we walk off the dais and because it's not Samoa, personal displays of affection are allowed and I don't need to pull my hand away, or pretend that every breathless fiber of my being isn't panting with happiness. Jackson is here. He's holding my hand. Walking beside me. And everything is right with the world.

CHAPTER
Twenty-One

SIX MONTHS LATER

*J*ackson is taking me to meet his family. In Texas. For the past month he's been asking me to go home with him because he says his parents want to meet me. I have successfully wriggled out of each invitation until now. I thought we would drive, but nope. We're flying.

"A private jet? Like some freaky Christian Grey sex plane? You have a private JET?! That's a joke right?" Heads turn at my raised shriek of a voice and Jackson has the grace to look embarrassed.

He takes my elbow and ushers me through the airport. "It's not mine. It's the company jet."

I give him an arched eyebrow of #ImNotStupid snark. "The company that has your name on it? The one called *Emory Steel?*"

He gives me a shrug and a half-grin, the kind that does delicious things to my insides and probably my outsides too. And then I forget what I was going to say next because we are whisked through check in and out onto the tarmac where a gleaming silver plane awaits us. A man in a suit welcomes us on board and shows us to our seats. There's plush carpet, and luxury features I've only ever seen on movies with Air Force One in them.

The pilot comes out to talk to Jackson and I give in to my agog curiosity, running my fingers along the gleaming interior and feeling the cushions.

"Madam, can I interest you in a drink?"

It's the man in a suit, holding a silver platter with two glasses of champagne on it. He reminds me of the butler in every British movie I've ever seen. My butler radar goes off even more when he gives me a little bow by way of introduction. "My name is Franklin, madam. I'm here to ensure you have an enjoyable flight. Anything at all, please let me know." Seeing my hesitation at the champagne, he adds smoothly, "We also have an extensive wine list, spirits, cocktails, and an assortment of juices. Of coffee perhaps? We have coffee from nearly every country in the world. We even have a beautiful roast blend from Samoa."

All the options are making my head spin. I give him a smile and ask for a Diet Coke. Playing it safe on my first time on a private jet. I won't be getting drunk on *this* flight with Jackson. I buckle up and grip the arm rests firmly, then turn when I feel Jackson's hand on mine.

"You okay?" he asks with soft concern in his eyes. "Franklin carries a range of meds if you need anything for anxiety."

I take a deep breath and wait for the familiar panic to bubble and build inside me as the plane starts its slow taxi down the runway. But it doesn't come. "I'm fine. So far anyway." I cant resist giving him a cheeky grin. "Hey, maybe I need to fly on a private jet everywhere I go from now on?"

Jackson quirks that familiar eyebrow at me. "Maybe you should. But not any random private jet. Just this one. Sitting next to me." He leans across to gently tug me closer, so he can capture my lips with his. A long, languorous kiss that lasts an eternity but is still all too fleeting. By the time the kiss ends, the plane is in the air and I didn't even realize it was taking off.

That's a pretty apt description for what the last six months have been like. A long, languorous kiss that lasts an eternity but is still too fleeting. Dating Jackson so far has been a constant adventure of discovery and at the same time, like finding the familiar, coming home. I keep waiting for the proverbial shoe to drop, for him to reveal his hidden axe murderer soul, because there must be something wrong with him, right? For him to be so utterly captivated by *me*? Because captivated is the best word for it. Jackson so far is the perfect boyfriend. Attentive, thoughtful and caring. I think I'm a rather spectacular girlfriend. If I do say so myself. He sends me flowers – just because it's Tuesday. I write him dirty sultry poetry and send it to him at work – just because it's Thursday. He has a fig honey pastry courier-delivered to my apartment where I'm holed up working on my next book – because he was at a restaurant meeting and came across a dessert that he was sure I would like to sample.

I had worried about trying to fit into Jackson's CEO billionaire lifestyle, the parties and glittering galas. But I quickly found that he didn't go to any, preferring instead to catch a movie, check out new restaurants and go dancing in dimly lit salsa clubs, jam packed with people who looked like us. "But I saw on your Facebook," I say to him. "All those photos of you at the fancy places with the fancy people?"

He shrugs. "That was my ex's crowd. I went along because it was important to her, but I wasn't comfortable. We didn't last long."

Our weekends are a combo of adrenaline-filled and lazy long days in bed. He's teaching me how to ride a motorbike. I'm teaching him how to bake cakes and how to speak Samoan. All the swear words first of course. We go to the library and I introduce him to all my favorite books. He promises to try and get to know them. Then he corners me behind the stacks and we have wild, furtive sex where he has to cover my mouth with his hand so I don't scream the place down and get banned for life from my happy place. After, I wait until we get outside and then demand with laughing severity, "What the hell was that?!"

"That was library sex," he says with a big smile. "Cross that off from the Scarlet and Jackson sex bucket list!"

"What bucket list? I didn't know anything about a sex list," I splutter indignantly. "We went there for the books. You said you wanted to read my favorites."

He tries to look repentant. "I did want to. But then I

saw how excited you get when you're talking about your favorite books, and you're just so fucking hot that I couldn't help myself. I must say, a library can be quite an arousing environment. You seemed to be quite aroused anyway." Innocence personified. "I didn't know libraries had that effect on you."

"It wasn't the library and you know it. It was you." I shake my head at him, laughing. "What else is on this list anyway? I should be briefed ahead of time so I can be prepared."

"It's a surprise. Wait and see!"

I take him to Sunday lunch at the Aunties house. They adore him as I knew they would. He thinks Nina is scary amazing especially after we go to watch her show. She thinks he's good for me. I am happy that my boyfriend and my best friend approve of each other.

I tell my sisters about him. Tamarina isn't surprised. She sends me a video of the children cheering and excited. Of Stella saying, "I knew it!" Naomi is in Washington D.C and pregnant. Morning sickness is making her life hell so her reaction is much more subdued. But Troy's cheerful teasing of his Best Man makes up for it.

I even tell Mother. She wants to know if they need to start collecting finances for a wedding. I roll my eyes at her from the safe distance and invisibility of Vegas.

Yes, the last few months have been perfect. I don't know

why we have to ruin it by going to meet his parents. They're going to hate me. I know how important his relationship with his parents is to Jackson. I don't know what will happen to us if they disapprove of us being together.

I'm getting anxious and he mistakes it for something else. He takes my hand in his, whispers, "Hey, it's okay. This plane has an impeccable safety record and my pilots are the best in the industry. The flight will be over before you know it."

I give him a weak smile. "I'm fine."

He kisses me again. The best way to cure my anxiety. I lean into him, wishing there were no barriers between us, an almost-whimper when the kiss ends. He holds me captive in his gaze, my face cradled in his hands. "I hate thinking about you being afraid on a plane anywhere. Without me."

"You do?" Why am I always a parrot stupidly repeating sentences whenever this man kisses me?

"I was worried about you. Back in Samoa, when you left suddenly like that? I kept thinking about you on those long flights back to Vegas without me by your side."

"You did?" I gulp.

His eyes speak truth and my heart is a gold medal ice skater doing a triple axle. He says, "Promise me you won't ever take off like that again? Without letting me know first?

Please?"

"I can't expect you to fly with me, every time I have to go somewhere," I laugh with a self-conscious little laugh and try to brush away his sincerity with a shrug and half-grin. But Jackson isn't dissuaded.

"Yes. But if you let me know in advance, I can have you take the jet wherever you need to go."

"I couldn't do that Jackson. Impose on you and your company like that. You can't spoil me with your kazillion dollar jet."

He frowns and his hold on me tightens as he tugs me close for another kiss. This time it's hungry and bold, a stamp of possession, fiery and scorching. It leaves me gasping for air. I have been well and truly marked by Jackson Emory and I like it. My inner independent woman falters and wilts before the onslaught. "We talked about this Scarlet. You are mine and I am yours. That means I get to spoil you with everything I have and everything that I am. Including my jet."

There's a finality to his tone that accepts no argument and so I shut up. That, and because Franklin chooses that moment to serve us a platter of divine looking treats. And a sinfully rich chocolate pie. We eat, sip champagne, and then Franklin retreats to wherever it is that private jet butlers go.

"Alone at last," Jackson murmurs in my ear, laying a

"Yes, really. It comes in handy on long haul flights. And it's perfect for distracting you from your anxiety over flying." Jackson is smiling as he carefully puts the pie down on the side table and then takes me in his arms for another air-stealing kiss. I groan and wilt into him, without planning to and he sweeps me up in his arms and carries me the remaining few steps to the bed.

Dimly I am aware of him laying me down, pausing to kick the door shut and snap the lock. My worry about Franklin walking in on us is immediately assuaged. I watch as he unbuttons his shirt. He doesn't take his eyes off me, not for a single moment, leaving his shirt on the floor as he comes to kneel above me.

"So all this is for my benefit?" I tease. "The jet and the bed? You naked? So I won't freak out about flying?"

He nods, grinning as he expertly unbuttons my shirt. "Of course. All for you and getting you through your flying anxiety. I'm willing to make whatever sacrifice is necessary. I've got moves that can help distract you."

"You've got moves? Are you sure?" I tease him. "I don't know. I was really enjoying that pie. Can't your moves wait until I'm done eating?"

He raises that eyebrow at me, fake poses and flexes above me so that every ridged contour on his torso, every chiseled cut and muscular ripple is calling out to me. "You'd rather have pie?!"

I adopt a disinterested air. "Of course. Wouldn't you? It is very good pie you know."

He gives me a dangerous smile and the message in his dark eyes has my pulse racing, going wild. "You're right. Let's have pie." Before I can decipher his intention, he reaches over and scoops a tantalizing glob of rich chocolate cream on his fingers, bringing it to my mouth. "Lick," he says.

I do it. Sucking his fingers clean of the husky sweetness, adding a little moan to tease him as I pretend to be sucking something else.

He gives me a low, throaty growl of appreciation. "Still prefer pie?"

I lick the last of the cream from his fingers and then lean back against the headboard. Calm and cool. "Of course. Can anything compare to a great chocolate pie?"

"We'll see," says Jackson. Expertly he unclips my bra, dips his fingers into the pie again, and this time, smears cream all over my breasts.

I yelp in surprise. "Jackson, it's cold!"

"Ohhh," he fakes regret. "I'm sorry. Let me fix that." He bends to take me in his mouth, eager and ravenous as he licks away every bit of chocolate, making no effort to quiet his hungry appreciation.

Whatever nonchalance I was faking, it's consumed in a dazed rush of sensual pleasure.

Two hours later I can confirm that the best cure for a fear of flying? Is Jackson and a chocolate cream pie.

CHAPTER
Twenty-Two

Jackson may have successfully distracted me from my flying anxiety, but there's not much he can do to stop me from panicking about meeting his parents. It's a long drive to their ranch. More than enough time for me to accelerate through all the possible scenarios of what can happen when they meet me.

"So they know I'm coming? You told them? About me?" I sound pitiful, even to myself. But I can't help it. I've never met parents before. Of a man I'm dating. I feel sick.

Jackson grins, reaches across the seat and takes my hand in his. "I told them enough."

What does that even mean? Enough?! "So they know I'm Samoan?" Code for – *they know I'm not white, right?* I think of Jackson's ex – the very blonde, very white woman.

"Of course," says Jackson. "They're looking forward to meeting you. My brothers Valk and Reno will be there. Valk is back from an assignment in Brazil and Reno is in between jobs right now."

"So I get to meet your brothers!" I try to sound cheerful about it but another gut wrench of nerves is making it trail of hot kisses down the line of my neck.

"Quit it," I laugh as I try to have another mouthful of pie. "You know my neck is ticklish!"

He growls, a delicious rumbling sound that starts low and deep in his chest, his fingers tip-toeing down my arm. "Okay. I'll kiss you elsewhere then." He takes my hand in his and proceeds to lick and suck on each one of my fingers. It has me gasping, both in delight and embarrassment as I look around for the staff.

"Stop it. What if Franklin sees?" I hiss.

"We have our privacy guaranteed." In one swift motion he unclips his seatbelt and stands.

"What are you doing?"

"Seatbelt sign is off, see?" says Jackson, pointing at the sign. "Come on, I haven't given you the tour."

"Wait, what about the pie? I haven't finished."

"We'll take it with us," he says, grabbing the dish in one hand as he pulls me along with the other.

"What's there to see on a jet anyway? Oh…" He leads me into a spacious cabin suite with a sprawling bed. It looks like we've walked into the presidential suite of a five star hotel and my *OHHHH WOW* is a long indrawn breath. "A bed? Really?"

difficult. As if meeting parents wasn't bad enough. I have to meet brothers too? How am I supposed to impress so many different people all at once? Never mind 'impress', how am I supposed to NOT embarrass myself in front of so many different people? I'm rambling now. "It'll be okay. They're used to you bringing your friends home all the time. It'll be casual and no big deal at all. Totally fine. Totally chill. No big deal…" Because I'm talking to myself more than to Jackson, I nearly miss his next words.

"Actually I don't."

"You don't what?" I say.

He's got his eyes on the road as he indicates to turn so I can't tell what sort of look he has on his face. "Bring friends home."

We pull up in front of an ornate gate with video camera surveillance and Jackson pushes a button on a gleaming dashboard. Then he turns to me with a smile that is a dusting of icing sugar on my soul.

"It'll be fine. You'll be fine."

"How do you know that?" I try not to whine but it's difficult. Breathing is difficult too. "What if I say the wrong things? Do the wrong things? Mess up?" What I don't say is – how can his parents possibly like me, when my own parents don't. *Ouch.*

He reaches across and draws me to him, kisses me.

Gentle, determined, soft and hard. Hungry and satisfying. How is it possible that this man's kisses can be all those things at once? When he pulls away, my lips feel swollen and I'm a mess. A thoroughly kissed and consumed mess. He cradles my face in his hands so that he can look deep into my eyes, so that I can't look away, so that all I can hear, see and feel is him. "Listen to me Scarlet. I love you. It won't matter what my family thinks of you. Nothing will change how I feel about you. The only people whose feelings matter in this? Are sitting here in this car right now. Okay?"

With that pronouncement, he starts up the truck again and we drive through the open gates, up a long driveway lined with sweeping oak trees. But I'm not looking at our surroundings, and nothing outside the truck is registering because for the first time, Jackson has said that he loves me.

Jackson loves me! OhmifuckingGosh, Jackson Emory loves me?!

Inside, my crazy Scarlet voice is screaming, I LOVE YOU TOO. FOREVER. ALWAYS. WITH ALL MY HEART. WITH EVERY MOLECULE OF MY BEING. I LOVE YOU SO MUCH THAT I WANT TO BREATHE THE SAME AIR AS YOU FOREVER.

Because yes, my inner Scarlet is pathetic.

Where before there didn't seem to be enough air, now there's an overabundance of oxygen because I'm floating, high, light as a cloud. A fluffy pavlova perfectly rising to pillowed perfection, spun sugar and whisked egg whites, golden brown edges, tips of divinity. That's where I am. Right next to Divinity. If my heart could sing it would be trilling at the top of its virtual lungs. If my feet could dance, I would be doing pirouettes and triple axles. I'm swept away on a fantasy fantastical vision.

Me and Jackson walking hand-in-hand on the beach. White sand and blue ocean. Me in a white dress. He's wearing a suit. There's frangipani petals fluttering in the air all around us, a cloud of perfumed perfection. Birds are singing. We're getting married, it's our perfect happy ending and we are walking into the sunset of all our happily ever after's. Just me and him. Jackson and Scarlet. Together forever. Nothing will ever part us. Ever ever ever…

"Scarlet? Are you coming?"

Huh, what? Oops, we're here.

Jackson is holding my door open and giving me a quizzical look because we've arrived and I'm sitting here in a daze like the silly woman that I am. In a love haze.

I scoot out of the car and trip over in my flustered haste. Jackson catches me and safe in his arms, we both laugh for a moment. I steal that moment to kiss him. A big sloppy hungry heated kiss because I'm so happy and in love and Jackson loves me and nothing can ruin this moment of perfection.

Nothing except for maybe an audience?

"Sheesh get a room you two!" says someone from somewhere behind us.

I freeze mid kiss and turn slowly. Jackson is grinning. "Scarlet, meet my brother Reno. The child who's never grown up."

There's a man standing on the front steps, leaning casually against one of the massive white columns, watching us, laughing at us. I want to die, shrivel up and wither in a heap of dust in the wind. I hiss at Jackson, "How could you let me do that? Why didn't you tell me he was there?!" Public displays of affection are the epitome of le-mafaufau'ness. The Samoan mortification is so strong that I nearly vomit. I have shamed my parents, my grandparents, my every ancestor back to Nafanua the war goddess. Kissing in public, IN FRONT OF YOUR BOYFRIEND'S FAMILY?! I am a harlot. A paumuku. A scarlet woman. Take me outside the city walls and stone me. I'll throw the first stone.

I am reminded of the time that our cousin Afeleki brought his palagi girlfriend home from Australia to meet the family. She would twine her arms around his neck and nibble on his ear, kiss his cheek at church. And the aunties would shudder in disgust and mutter behind their woven fans about her behavior of Biblical whoredom. Even we children would know she was acting in shameful filthy ways. When Afeleki came next time to Samoa – alone – everyone nodded sagely and congratulated him on his wisdom and blessed escape from the clutches of a girl with no morals, no parents, no alofa.

Yet look at me. Here now I was behaving just like Afeleki's palagi girlfriend. Which was a greater sin because unlike her, I was Samoan and had been taught the right path. I was supposed to know better.

Way to make a good first impression Scarlet.

Jackson goes to hug his brother with a few more cracks about spying on consenting adults.

Reno laughs. "You already gave us a free show on the video monitor."

I give both men a questioning look. *What video monitor?*

"You know, at the front gate? You buzzed? Elizabeth went to check the camera and we all got an eyeful." He advances with an open laughing face, hand outstretched. "Hi Scarlet. Welcome to the family ranch. We're all excited to meet you."

I shake his hand but I'm shriveled inside, because of what he's just said. *Jackson's mother saw us kissing on the video camera?* This keeps getting worse. Can a tornado please happen right now and take me to Kansas?

Jackson puts a reassuring arm around me and gives me a gentle squeeze. "Cut it out Reno, you're not helping Scarlet's worries about meeting our crazy family. Don't scare my girlfriend off before she's even gotten inside." It's said lightheartedly with a smile but there's an undertone of warning and Reno responds to it immediately.

"I'm kidding, Scarlet. Sorry. We do it to each other all the time. I don't get to see Jackson enough and I have a few weeks worth of sibling roasting to catch up on," says Reno.

I seize on his words with grateful relief. "So Mrs. Emory didn't see us at the front gate? Being inappropriate?"

Reno gives me a quizzical look, then shoots a glance at Jackson. The men exchange words without saying anything and Jackson's brother is chastened. "No she didn't. I assure you. I'm the one who answered the buzzer. Elizabeth was busy in the kitchen. Come through. Everyone's waiting to meet you."

I give Jackson a desperate look of pleading and he reads my mind. Because he loves me and he's brilliant of course. He takes my hand and escorts me inside. "Scarlet why don't you take a few minutes to freshen up first? Guest bathroom is through here. Then come join us in the kitchen through that hall, okay?"

I'm weak with relief. The last thing I want is to meet Jackson's parents while I'm a kissed-up mess. I do what I have to do in the bathroom, including going through the breathing exercises my therapist taught me. *There, now I feel ready.* Or as ready as I will ever be. Let's do this.

I walk through rooms and my jaw drops open at the splendid beauty of the family's home. I follow the voices and find everyone in a massive open plan kitchen and dining area.

"Here she is – everyone, meet Scarlet," says Jackson as he takes my hand in his, ushering me forward. "Come meet my parents first."

Before I can take another step, a human tornado rushes forward and envelops me in a bone crushing hug. She smells like mint and lemons and there's sunshine in her smile as she steps back to look me up and down. "Let me look at you! I did try stalking you on Facebook but nothing compares to the real thing, right here in my kitchen!"

Wait, what – she stalked me on Facebook? Oh shit. Who does that? What kind of mother does that?

HANDS UP ANYONE WHOSE MOTHER HAS STALKED THEIR GIRLFRIEND ON FACEBOOK?! HELP! RED ALERT. SEND HELP.

Elizabeth is not what I envisioned at all. Jackson had told me she'd been the driving force behind Emory Steel before her retirement, and I'd imagined her as this tall, crisp, cool Chanel suited woman with an iron handshake and a severe chignon. But instead she's a short, messy figure in denim overalls and a riot of curls barely contained in a pink scrunchie. There's splotchy stains on her apron.

I'm introduced to the others. Jackson's father Mark. His brother Valk. Elizabeth waves me to sit at the countertop while she continues working at the bench. "I'm making mojitos. The best thing on a hot Texas day. The mint is from my garden. Here, drink up."

A tall glass of icy cool deliciousness is pushed into my hands and I take a long sip appreciatively. "Hmmm this is lovely. Thank you."

"It's good, yes?!" Elizabeth gives the others a look of triumph. "I told you she would like my mojitos." Back to me, she continues talking, a hundred words a minute, rolling her *Rrrrrr's* and drawling her *Aaaaaaaa's*. "These boys, so know-it-all. They said I should ask you what you want to drink, give you a selection of cocktails, but I told them, who can not love my mojitos? Thank you for proving me right to these boys. As usual." A laugh. "But then I have to confess, I did see on your Instagram that you liked a good mojito."

OhmifuckingGoodness she's been through my Instagram too? Is no social media app safe from this woman? (Let this be a lesson to you all, good readers – put your apps on private. Right now.) I'm trying to think what I shared on Snapchat lately and whether or not I need to be apologizing pre-emptively for anything unsavory.

Reno is helping in the kitchen and places a platter of tortilla chips in front of us. "I apologize for our mother Scarlet," he says, shaking his head with a mournful frown. "Jackson should have warned you. She's infamous for her social media stalking. None of her children, or their friends are ever safe."

The men share a laugh and Valk adds, "She's gotten a bit better though. Remember when she first got on Facebook and she didn't understand the difference between private message and posting comments on our pictures?"

Jackson and his brothers burst out laughing. "I forgot about that," says Jackson. He explains for my benefit. "We were in Junior year of high school. Elizabeth had me make her a Facebook. She thought she knew everything about how to use it. She saw a girl post a photo of herself on Valk's page."

His brother jumps in, "An innocent, completely rated G photo! And Elizabeth put her on public blast. It was a girl in my class and I was humiliated."

Elizabeth makes a snort of disbelief and raises her hand to pause the conversation. "Scarlet, let me tell you the real story. I'm scrolling down the page and what do I see? A photograph of a near naked girl sitting on a bed in a seductive pose, and she's commented, 'Missing you Valk.' Now I ask you, what would you have done as a mother?"

The Samoan in me knows exactly what to say, but Valk interrupts again, "She wasn't naked! She was wearing a nude colored bra. Nothing seductive about the picture at all."

The brothers are fake jostling each other in the kitchen now, with sideways grins. It's obvious this is a favorite family story and source of much good-natured banter.

Elizabeth sniffs and adopts an air of righteousness. "All I did was write a simple comment on the photo. Nothing for anyone to get upset about at all."

Her husband joins the conversation now, a glass in hand

and placing an arm around his wife's shoulders. "Now dear, lets not tell lies in front of our guest." He says to me, "Elizabeth asked Valk on his Facebook page, where the young woman's clothes were, and that his mother didn't give him permission to have naked pictures on his Facebook. Apparently all the boys friends saw it and there was much talk about it at their school."

"To be fair, I didn't realize everyone could see my comment," interrupted Elizabeth. "So a public blast wasn't my intention."

"Yes, but how do you explain all the other times you destroyed us on Facebook?" asks Reno, with an exaggerated aggrieved air. "Like when you told Jackson his hair looked like our dog's tail?"

More laughter from everyone and now even I'm smiling as I relax slightly. This family is nothing like mine. Sure there's sarcasm and teasing, but it doesn't have the barbed sting or the whispers behind it like it does back home. Maybe, this visit wont be so bad after all?

"Mrs. Emory can I help you with the food preparation?" I ask, getting up from my seat and ready to do kitchen chores. If there's anything I feel confident about doing, its working in the kitchen.

All the men laugh and I throw Jackson a look of confusion. *Did I say something wrong?*

Jackson shakes his head and gives me a smile of

reassurance. "Never mind us Scarlet. We're laughing because Elizabeth doesn't cook. The apron is just for show."

"Yeah, Mark is the cooking maestro in this family," explains Ronan. "Our mother cook dinner? Never!"

"I make great cocktails," protests Elizabeth as she joins in the laughter. "And the apron is needed for chopping the mojito mint, so there."

Mark gives his wife a look of undisguised fondness. "You do make great cocktails darling." To me he says, "Thanks for the offer Scarlet but everything's done and the boys will dish it up for us. Lets go to the table shall we?"

We move to a huge carved oak dining table. Jackson and his brothers bring platters of food to the table while the conversation continues. Now they are reminiscing about the few times Elizabeth tried her hand at cooking, with disastrous consequences. Burnt pies, charred hams, and stews so salty that, "Even our hogs wouldn't eat it!" More laughter.

"I learnt a long time ago that one should know their strengths and weaknesses," says Elizabeth with a grin. "Then work to them. Me and cooking have never been friends, so I figure, why force it? Early in our marriage Mark figured out that if he wanted to eat anything edible then he needed to be the family chef. When I got back from the office, he would have a beautiful dinner ready for us, and I only had to make the cocktails. The perfect partnership."

We eat dinner and it's delicious. Golden cornbread that crumbles perfectly and melts in your mouth. Rich savory chili with the right amount of spicy kick. A platter of corn on the cob, crisp and sweet with melted butter and salt. Green salad made with tomatoes and lettuce from Mark's vegetable garden. But even better than the meal, is the conversation. There's lots of laughter and good-natured teasing. Perhaps Jackson has warned them of my anxiety, but whatever the reason, the family doesn't subject me to any intense scrutiny and the interrogation is gentle. A few light questions.

"So Scarlet, you're a writer?" asks Mark as he passes me more cornbread.

"Yes, I write romance novels." I've been practicing saying that without cringing and I'm getting better at it. *Be proud Scar dammit.* I'm ready for jokes and snide cracks about writing trash. Reno and Valk are nudging each other with sly grins and I give them my most icy smile. The one that says – *I am strong and resolute. You can't make me embarrassed for writing romance.*

"Yeah Elizabeth, she writes romance novels," says Reno loudly. "Do you want to say something right about now? Have you anything to share?"

The boys are trying not to laugh and Jackson looks as puzzled as I am. *What's going on?*

"Oh stop it boys. You're making Scarlet uncomfortable." To me, Elizabeth says, "As soon as Jackson told us you're an author, I went and looked for your books on Amazon."

Oh fuck. "You did?"

Valk leaps in, "She bought them all. And after she read them, she ordered paperbacks and she's got them here for you to sign."

"But only if you don't mind," says Mark smoothly. "You certainly don't need to."

"We told her she shouldn't pester you," says Reno with a grin. "But she loved your books and she's dying to ask you about them."

Well I sure didn't expect this. "I'm thrilled you enjoyed them," I say to Elizabeth.

"I did," says Elizabeth. "I don't get to read for pleasure very often but once I started one of your books, I couldn't put them down."

She gets her copies of my books and I sign them at the table while the men continue to tease her about being a fangirl. I had brought a dessert and everyone says many complimentary things about the pecan pie as Elizabeth quizzes me about my books, my writing process, and my characters. The time flies and before I know it, its time for us to go.

There's a few minutes where Elizabeth and I are alone in the hall while Jackson is saying goodbye to his father and brothers. She gets a serious look on her face and I steel myself for whatever she has to dish out. *This is it.* All the niceness before was a front and here, now she's going to tell me to stay away from her son, that I'm not good enough for him.

But no.

"I'm so glad Jackson brought you to meet us," she says. "He never brings anyone home."

"Thank you for making me feel so welcome," I say, touched.

"He's been through a lot and he's come far," says Elizabeth. "We're so very proud of him, the man he's become. The son that he is to us. The big brother that he is to the others." And then so softly I almost think I imagine it, she adds, "And the husband that he will be one day." She surprises me with a hug. "I hope you come again to visit us Scarlet."

CHAPTER
Twenty-Three

As we drive out from the Emory Ranch, Jackson asks, "Do you mind if we take a detour first before we head back to the airport?"

"Sure." I am happy. Buzzing about how successful the meeting with his family had been. "I really liked that. You have a great family Jackson."

He smiles, with his eyes still on the road. We have turned off the main road and now are climbing on a winding side road. "You sure? We can be a little crazy sometimes. And Elizabeth is the firecracker that we revolve our crazy around. She can be overwhelming for some people. I hope you were okay?"

"Of course. I like her. She's funny. And she loves her sons very much."

"You should see us when all the boys are home," says Jackson. "Then it really gets rowdy. We used to fight all the time when we were kids. When we each first came to the family. Mark used to call us a pack of wolves, scrapping over every insult, imagined or otherwise. We're grown now so we're civilized somewhat."

"It's beautiful to see your parents together," I continue. Wistful as I think about my own parents. "They love each other so openly. It's great."

"I don't know. They could use some Samoan reservedness when it comes to all the smooching, I reckon," he jokes. "Nobody likes to see their parents getting so touchy-feely with each other in the kitchen."

The truck comes to a halt. "We're here," says Jackson. He gets out and comes round to open my door.

I look around with interest. We are at the top of a ridge, a hill. Down below is a long valley. The sun is setting and the sky is alight with fire and pink ruffles. There's a lone tree here at the top of the hill, a massive oak. Underneath it's shade, is a solitary wrought iron bench set in a stone block. Jackson reaches out his hand. "Come sit with me a while?"

We sit side by side and look out over the valley. There's a soft breeze and the call of distant birds far overhead. "All that is Emory Ranch," explains Jackson. "My grandfather – Mark's father – started it from next to nothing and slowly built it up over the years, before handing it over to his son. I never met him. He died before Mark and Elizabeth adopted me. He planted this tree though. According to Emory family lore, he proposed to his wife here, and planted the oak tree when she said yes. When Mark asked Elizabeth to marry him, he brought her here to this spot. That's why he had this bench put in. See?" Jackson stands so he can point out the names inscribed on the stone beneath our feet.

Lincoln and Deborah
Mark and Elizabeth

Beside each pair of names is a date.

This is a beautiful story and a beautiful spot. But I'm confused. Why did Jackson bring me here? Why is he telling me all this? There's a buzzing of warning inside my head.

Something's happening. Something's coming.

"Growing up on the ranch as a teenager, I always said I would propose to my future wife here as well. Inscribe our names right here alongside those of my parents and grandparents. Sure all us boys are adopted, but Mark and Elizabeth always treated us like we were their own, they made sure we knew that this legacy and heritage belonged to all of us." Jackson takes a deep breath and kneels down in front of me. Slips a velvet box from his pocket. "Scarlet, you know pretty much everything about me. Where I've been and what I've done. Things I'm not proud of, and things that got me holding my head up high. I know I don't have the ancestry and heritage that you do, I don't bring the strength of a vast vibrant family tree to the table, I'm not Samoan. But I love you and I offer all that I am and all that I have, with the added promise of all that we can be, together. Will you marry me?"

He opens the box and offers me a ring of diamond fire . Kneeling before me under the Texas sky, he is steadfast, sure and true.

I can't breathe. Shock chokes me. Fear cripples me. Sadness pierces me, a knife of piercing guilt. The moment of truth has arrived and I'm not ready. "I can't. I want to, but I can't."

He's confused. "What do you mean? Why not?"

"I can't have children," I blurt out, then turn away quickly so I won't see his reaction. "You know what happened to me when I was a child. I got pregnant when I was fourteen. Mother didn't want anyone to find out, especially not Father. Abortion is illegal in Samoa so she took me to someone who could take care of it secretly."

"What happened?" prompts Jackson.

"There was an infection. I got sick. Real bad. My mother panicked, tried to put off taking me to the hospital for as long as possible. I ended up in critical condition, it was touch and go for awhile. They had to remove my uterus, all my baby-growing and storage facility," I explain with a touch of lightness but he doesn't smile. There's a darkness in his eyes that I can't read.

"I'm sorry Scarlet," he says, reaching out to hold my hand. "No child should have to go through that."

"I should have told you a long time ago. Full disclosure and all that. But I was scared. So yeah, you should know I'm damaged goods. Faulty merchandise." I wince at my own miserable attempt at humor.

"Anything else you want to tell me?" asks Jackson. "Any more secrets you want to share?"

I shake my head.

A ghost of a grin as he stands, tugging me up to stand with him. Close enough so he can reach out and lightly slip his hand behind my neck, gently bracing me as he bends to place a single kiss on my forehead. "I love you," he says. "So I'm asking again, now that you've told me your final secret, will you marry me?"

There are treacherous tears betraying me now. A half sob as I say, "I love you too Jackson. So much that it hurts to ever think of losing you. But you have such a great family, you've got it all together. And I'm a mess. I've dealt with a lot of my baggage and I'm proud of where I'm at. But it's still me."

He cradles my face in his big, warm hands and bends to delicately kiss the tear stains on my cheek. "Scarlet, I was a crack baby. In and out of the system from the age of five, never sure when my mother would show up or when she would disappear. On the streets by the time I was twelve, stealing, vandalism, on a one way road to nowhere when Mark and Elizabeth found me and took me in. You know all these things and yet you still accept me. We're all damaged, faulty in some way. It's how we fill in the cracks. What we do with the broken pieces. My past made me who I am today. Just as yours has refined you into all that you are now. All that I love."

"But what about children?" I demand.

"What about them?" he replies. "A woman isn't a baby-making machine and I don't love you for your eggs and future children. Or your lack of them."

"But you're a man and you'll want…offspring…sons… an heir…someone to carry on your name, your family line," I splutter.

The arched eyebrow conveys his disbelief. "We're not in medieval England or some ridiculous bloodline movie. I'm one of five sons adopted by my parents. I carry their name with pride. When they retired, they handed the company over to me. Not because I was the oldest, but because I'm the only one who was interested in the engineering and construction field. You don't need a bloodline to carry on one's family name or business or ensure the future. I don't want offspring – I want you. I want to wake up with you every morning, and watch sunsets like this with you. Have adventures with you, and then stay in bed for two days straight with you, savouring chocolate pie together in the best way possible…"

"So you don't want kids?"

A shrug. "I want you. If we decide one day that we want a baby then we'll get one. Two, three, four – however many you want. There's surrogacy, adoption and foster children. You forget, I'm very rich Scarlet. I can give you almost anything, or at least spend an insane amount to try. There's amazing advances in science happening every day, womb transplants, whatever. If that's what you want, then we'll research it. I would get any and all of those options for you."

"Really?"

"Yes. But right here, right now? I'm not interested in the possibility of our imaginary children. I'd rather not have any here right now. Because then I couldn't do this…" And then he's kissing me. Fierce and hungry, he tastes like the ocean. Wild, windswept and with a bite of salt, my tears.

"There's one more thing I have to say." I take a deep breath. "We're not in a romance novel Jackson."

He grins, gives me the eyebrow raise. "Umm I think I know that."

"I'm not the star of a plus-sized novel who meets a sexilicious man that can see the true beauty of her skinny inner self and adores her through the blubber, and then she magically loses weight because she's finally found love and he 'completes' her. There isn't a skinny Scarlet waiting to bust out. I'm not going to stop eating because we're married, I'm not going to take up running, or kayaking or suddenly train for an Ironman and become a toned version of myself with rippling muscles and more abs than you. This is me. All of this." I slap at my thighs and then grab handfuls of my love handles. "I'm not gonna change. It's taken me a long time to love myself, exactly as I am. And I can't be with you if there's a chance that you're waiting, hoping for me to stop stuffing my face with dessert, so that I'll emerge from my chrysalis looking like a brown Barbie butterfly."

A long pause.

"Are you done?" he asks. "I've listened to you and now, it's your turn to listen to me. Can you do that?"

I nod.

His voice is strong, sure and deep. "I mean it Scarlet." He takes my hand in his. "Listen to me, I'm going to be brutally honest with you."

Oh hell. I don't want to hear this. You idiot Scar, honesty is overrated!

"You're right, this isn't a romance novel or a Disney fairy-tale. When I first met you on that plane ride from turbulence hell I didn't fall instantly in love with you. No, there was nothing romantic about how I felt sitting next to you for six hours. That plane ride was torture for me too. But not for the same reasons as you. I wasn't falling in love with you and I certainly didn't know anything about your inner beauty." He takes a deep breath. "I was rock hard and crazy lusting for you."

Shock drives away tears as I stare up at him open-mouthed. *WTF?!*

"Excuse me?" my voice is trembling and I can't breathe properly. "What did you say?"

"It's crude I know but we're being honest with each other. No secrets. No lies." A wry grin. "That day on the plane – I wanted you. More than I've ever wanted any woman before. You were a hot mess with that red flower – a hibiscus I think? – in your hair, a tangled jungle about your face. You fell into my lap and then looked up at me with those dark liquid eyes a man could drown in. And that mouth..." He brings a hand up to caress the curve of my cheek and rubs the pad of his thumb against my bottom lip. There's a dangerous gleam in his eyes as he mutters throatily, so low I almost don't catch the words, "I looked down at you kneeling between my legs and I couldn't tear my eyes away from these lips, this mouth and all its promise. Instant rush of blood to places I'd rather not have it rush to. Not when I'm confined in close quarters on plane, with no way to alleviate the pressure."

"You were out of breath like you'd been running and sweat had your top clinging to your perfect lushness, and I wanted to touch you. Like this." His hands, deft and knowing, move to cup and caress through the fabric of my shirt, and the rush of pleasure is like the sweet shock of a first bite into a chocolate mint ice cream cake. *Oww, cold mint shot to the brain...more please.*

He continues. "The way you ate those savouries like they were manna from heaven. You had your eyes closed, one finger in your mouth as you sucked a stray lick of sauce. That little moan of contentment, it was like watching a foodgasm. Thinking about it now is driving me nuts." His voice catches at the memory and with a muttered oath, he pulls me to him, grinding into me so every turgid part of me is in full frontal contact with every thrilling part of him.

Just like that, this romantic nature proposal scene changes into the lusty thrill of a moment straight out of an erotic novel. He's breathing hard as he kisses the line of my neck, a nip and bite of sweet pain that has me gasping in the evening air. There's a primal serrated edge to him, the flame burn of chilli chocolate… *fighting not to bite too much because you know you'll burn your mouth, but wanting so bad to unleash your control anyway.*

He's on edge. And knowing that, seeing that – it's a heady sensation of power and passion. *Hot daaayum. I got this man on a sex cliff-edge. Me. Fatgirl me!*

"When you ate those pastries, there were tiny flecks of sauce on your mouth – and I wanted to lick them away, like this." He bends to lave his tongue along my bottom lip and then suckle before dipping into my mouth, tasting, caressing, searching, playing in a kiss that leaves me scorching with need. I moan a little in disappointment when he pulls away.

"You did?" I whisper huskily. "You wanted to kiss me on the plane? Really?"

His eyes are dark and uncompromising. "You're not listening to me Scarlet."

"I'm not?" He's not touching me anymore and I want him to. So bad. So bad I could burst with wanting.

Like Ovocné Knedlíky. Czech dumplings bursting ripe with

plum and peach jam. Made of potato and curd that cooks up doughy and soft, served warm and jam-stuffed with deliciousness.

He shakes his head and there's a rough severity in his tone. "No, you're not listening. I didn't want to *kiss* you on that flight to Hawaii. I wanted to fuck you."

His unexpected roughness, has me breathless. *Who knew the F-word could feel so good?*

"I wanted to make hot, sweet love to you," he says. "Over. And. Over. Again. Why do you think I took my jacket off and put it in my lap?"

"Ummm, I don't know. Because you were hot and you needed air?" The words sound pitiful even to me.

His eyes, they reprimand me as he takes my hand and guides it to the hard throbbing length of him. "No, because I needed to hide how much I wanted you. That's how hard I was, that's how bad I wanted you then, and how I want you now."

"Oh." *Oh indeed.* Excitement has me fumbling at the fastening of his jeans but he laughs – deep and rumbling – and pulls away, takes my hands and pins them lightly behind me.

"Then, when I saw you at that birthday party, so beautiful in that green dress, the arc of your hip, the curve of this …" He holds my hands with one of his so he can run the other down the side of my body, down, down. "Hmmm," he breathes against my hair, "such a beautiful ass."

My knees turn to custard and go limp as I breathe a little whimpering sigh. He doesn't let me fall though. He presses against me and I cling to his sure earthbound strength. "When you danced with me, when I put my hands on your waist, your skin burned me through the fabric of your dress but I wanted more. I wanted to do this..." He takes firm hold of my shirt and with one abrupt motion, he rips the fabric in two. A jagged tearing sound almost as loud as my surprised exclamation.

"Oh!" *OhmyfreakinHeck...*

I'm bared to the evening air, to the fire of his gaze. *Thank heaven I wore the black lace bra.*

I squirm, trying to cover up again but he growls at me, a low throaty "No" and so I freeze, poised in mortification. He bends to rain kisses on me, setting delicious fire to my hips, the rounded curve of my belly. I melt some more. Especially when he murmurs against my hot skin, "I love your softness. Can't get enough of you." I run my fingers through his hair as he kisses a trail upwards.

He's still talking. Still razing my every particle with his words of worshipful awe. "Going to the beach with you was the hardest though. When that wave knocked you over and I pulled you out of the surf, laughing that magnificent laugh of yours? Remember that?"

He has me sitting on the bench now, so he can sink to his

knees, between my parted legs, and he's holding me captive in his gaze, willing me to listen, while his hands are at work – compelling me to believe. I moisten my lips and nod. *Yes I remember that day.* Then he slowly peels down the lace cups of my brasserie and he's doing things with his hands that send feather dustings of feeling all over me, confectioner's sugar, sweet and tempting.

From far away, I hear someone sigh a little half-moaning sound. I think it's me. But I can't be sure, not when Jackson's hands are playing, plumping and tugging. From far away, I hear him say, "You were all wet in the salt-ocean, your shirt was soaked through and clinging to these, the most glorious breasts I'd ever seen, a wet T-shirt contest winner right here." He laughs, low and throaty and just that sound alone has me whimpering weak with desire. "I wanted nothing more than to lick every drop of salt ocean from your skin." He bends to replace his hands with his hot, wet mouth and I'm gasping. It's so incredibly good that I never want him to stop.

I try to find my voice. It's swimming through thick puddles of chocolate sauce and navigating hazelnut pralines. "Ummm, so what you're saying is, that you didn't notice my fabulous personality at all?"

A raspy growl of laughter as he raises his head. There's a wicked gleam in his eyes as he imprisons me in his arms. "Sure I did. Like the night of the bridal shower when you were Ursula the Octopus Witch. Your inner goddess was on full display then," he teases, with a soft kiss to my forehead. He turns serious. "I watched you in the club, before you realized I was there. Everyone else dressed like Disney princesses and yet doing their best to radiate sex. Then there was you in that sea witch outfit, vibrant, fearless, unapologetic, boldly being you. You were amazing. I'll admit the beauty of your inner self got to me that night." He's back to teasing and I relish it. "It almost distracted me from wanting to do this…"

In a replay of that unforgettable night, he slides up the folds of my skirt, tugging aside the lace thong. He looks up at me with taut teasing desire in his eyes. "I know I'm supposed to be focusing on your soul, the inner butterfly – but I find your body insanely distracting."

Then he's hooking my right thigh over his shoulder so I'm half-sitting on his broad shoulder, so I'm open and welcoming, so I can't hide from him – even if I wanted to.

But let's face it. I don't want to.

Not when he's taking a decadent satisfaction in wreaking magic with his tongue. Not when I'm leaning back with my arms splayed on the bench, arching my spine, thrusting and needy, caught in a swirling jagged maelstrom of feeling, pulsating light and sound. Not when I'm not thinking about dessert, *not once* – because I'm not thinking at all.

I'm racing towards a cliff-edge, about to leap and soar – but then he stops. Pauses to look up at me, "Still worried I'm not in love with your body Scarlet?"

Eyes fly open in dismay. *Nooo! Don't stop. He's so mean. I can't believe he's torturing me like this."*

"Yes. I mean no, I'm not worried..." I can barely get the words out and he grins in triumph before resuming his beautiful torture.

This time, there's no stopping. This time, I leap and soar – and he is with me on every tremulous breath as if he's a liquid force pulsating through my veins. When the world stops spinning and the ground settles beneath my feet, it's to find myself secure in his arms as he holds me, steadies and soothes me.

There isn't a dessert on the planet that can come close to describing how perfect it is to be in Jackson's arms, right here, right now in this moment.

"I'm sorry to have to break it to you. You got it backwards," he says softly. "I didn't fall in love with your inner beauty and *then* want to make love to you. Truth is, I wanted to have hot, dirty sex with you from the moment we met – and falling in love with the rest of you had to catch up with my raging hard-on."

I'm delighted. Sure most girls want to hear their man loves them for their personality...their insides...their essential inner beauty and 'it's not about the physical, I promise!' But not me. Not this fat girl. Not right now anyway. I want to hear all about how much he longs for me, and yes, how raging his hard-on really is. I smile up at him weakly, "So what you're telling me, is that you want to marry me for my body?"

"Absolutely," he says. His voice is raspy sandpaper that sears my skin and my soul. "I promise to spend the rest of my life in utter worship and adoration of your body. As it is now, ten years from now, fifty years from now." There's no more teasing as he cups my face gently, so gently – in his hands. There's only total intensity and naked intent. Resolution. "And I promise to spend a thousand lifetimes learning and loving all the mysterious, beautiful layers of the inner secret butterfly Scarlet." There's that wicked grin again. "I'm pretty sure she's not skinny though."

"Yeah?" I whisper.

"Mmhmm," he says, "I'm pretty sure the inner secret Scarlet, wherever she's hiding – is just as abundant," he punctuates each word with a lingering kiss, "luscious, complex, frustrating, magnificent, and perfect, as the woman I'm wildly, impossibly in lust and in love with already."

Now if that isn't a declaration of true love, then I don't know what else is.

"I believe you," I say. "Who knew that an engineer could be so poetic?"

An arched eyebrow. "I don't think it's my poetry that persuaded you. Pretty sure it was my dirty hot sex moves."

Oops. Busted.

I hide my face in his shirt, against his chest as he laughs

but then I remember there's not much point trying to be all dignified now. Not when I'm a wild mess and my shirt is in tatters.

I raise my eyes to meet his. "Who says there's no poetry in steamy, dirty hot sex?"

We share a smile and then he asks, "So does this mean you're saying yes? Now that I've seduced you?"

"Yes. I will marry you. But on one condition."

"What is it?"

"We have to elope. No crazy Samoan wedding drama for us. Deal?" I say.

His face lights up. Raw happiness. "Now *that*, is the best deal I've ever been offered. You got it."

He kisses me under a vast sky, as the sun slips beyond the horizon, and the tapestry of night unfolds. Wind rustles the leaves of the great oak tree, a soft whispering. And his kiss, it makes the stars dance.

This, this is our happy ending. Finally. And the beginning of our forever.

I have crossed the troubled sea. I have turned my face to the sun.

At night, I have the constellations to guide me. The Ulimasao of my god to power me forward. The fierce wisdom of my ancestors to stoke the fire within me. The steel strength and spirit of all those who love me, to bear me up.

I am Scarlet, a daughter descended of Nafanua and I am silent no more. No lies, no secrets. I am no longer afraid. To fight. To live, laugh and love. To hope.

And yes, to forgive.

The End

ACKNOWLEDGMENTS

Faafetai lava to all the readers of Scarlet's story who have waited patiently for her happy ending – yes I know it took a while, but I hope you find the wait was worth it.

In September 2015, my beloved second mother passed away. Somewhat adrift on the journey of grief, I shut down all my author projects at the time, including Scarlet's conclusion, and took a two-year hiatus from writing fiction. It was a much needed break and one in which I exercised different writing and editing muscles, but it's been a joy returning to the magic of storytelling. Peka, although you're gone, your love continues to find its way into my writing, your fierce spirit and strength (and even your cooking) is in my books. I miss you.

I pay tribute to the many survivors of child sexual abuse who have shared their stories with me. I am awed and humbled by your courage, strength and resilience. To you I say, we are not broken. And our voice, hurt and healing is always more important than our family and our community's pride and reputation. My prayer is that all survivors will find the love and support they need to help them through their own particular journeys across troubled seas.

Love and light to dear friends who have walked with me through many adventures and challenges, who ensure that I do get out of the hermit cave once in a while

Thank you to Darren and my children for all your encouragement and support of my writing. You make stories happen.

Lani

ABOUT THE AUTHOR

Lani Young is a Samoan/Maori author and columnist. The 2018 ACP Pacific Laureate (selected by the African, Caribbean, Pacific Group of States), she is the author of 11 books including the international bestselling TELESA series. She's worked as a scriptwriter for Disney, and her stories for children are published by the NZ School Journal.

When she's not writing romance, Lani writes about feminism, culture, parenting, climate justice, gender, and everything in between. Her writing on child sexual abuse and domestic violence in Pasifika communities has generated dialogue in many forums worldwide. She is also an award-winning journalist.

Lani lives in Samoa and New Zealand with her husband and five children.

You can find more of her writing at her blog: Sleepless in Samoa.

Sign up to her newsletter and get the latest on her new book releases, bonus stories, and author events: Lani Young Newsletter

IF YOU ENJOYED THIS BOOK

THEN YOU SHOULD CHECK OUT THESE OTHER AUTHORS OF PASIFIKA

Secret Shopper

Tanya Taimanglo

After moving to California from the tropical island of Guam, Phoenix Farmer's marriage to her high school sweetheart, Bradley unravels. Forced to find a job, she retreats into the world of SECRET SHOPPING and thrives. As Phoenix discovers her true self without Bradley, she becomes an unwilling goddess with the help of her best friend Rachel. She snags the attention of Thomas-the creative, handsome and persistent target she has been assigned to evaluate. Can she hold off Thomas's charm until her divorce becomes final? What will she decide when her father falls ill unexpectedly and pulls her back to Guam? This romantic comedy will have you cheering for Phoenix as she rises from the ashes and becomes a shinier version of her former self.

Scar of the Bamboo Leaf

Sieni A.M.

"That boy is like the bamboo...foreign and unknown in this environment. But like the bamboo, if you plant and nurture it in the right soil, it has the potential to grow vibrant and strong."

Walking with a pronounced limp all her life has never stopped fifteen-year-old Kiva Mau from doing what she loves. While most girls her age are playing sports and perfecting their traditional Samoan dance, Kiva finds serenity in her sketchbook and volunteering at the run-down art center her extended family owns, nestled amongst the bamboo.

When seventeen-year-old Ryler Cade steps into the art center for the first time, Kiva is drawn to the angry and misguided student sent from abroad to reform his violent ways. Scarred and tattooed, a friendship is formed when the gentle Kiva shows him kindness and beauty through art, until circumstances occur beyond their control and they are pulled away.

Immersed in the world of traditional art and culture, this is the story of self-sacrifice and discovery, of acceptance and forbearance, of overcoming adversity and finding one's purpose. Spanning years, it is a story about an intuitive girl and a misunderstood boy and love that becomes real when tested.

Gravity
The Michaels Family Book 1

Tracey Poueu-Guerrero

Eva Michaels has been groomed for greatness on the field and on the court. Her four brothers have trained her and molded her into one of the top female athletes in California. Oblivious to her beauty, she hides behind the tomboy with her routine. Until the day she meets the emerald-eyed Dream-Boy who saves her from a hazing at the hands of the neighborhood bully.

Colton Banks never looks back when his mother moves him across the states. He meets the Michaels, the family next door. He quickly becomes part of the family and the only friend that Eva Michaels has ever had. He is captivated by her. He's never met anyone like her. As kids, being friends was easy because Eva's brothers were always around as a buffer. As teenagers, they fight hard to suppress their attraction as they struggle to maintain, at times, an awkward friendship.

College changes everything. They both accept scholarships to Stanford and for the first time in her life, Eva is living life without the security blanket she grew up with. Her brothers. At first, they try to keep things simple and remain "just friends." But the temptation becomes too great. Their passion undeniable. The harder they try to fight it; the more powerful becomes the pull towards each other. Colton longs to take their relationship to the next level but fears he may push Eva away for good. Eva is besieged with longing and aches to be Colton's. She can't quite come to grips with how strong her desire for him truly is. Unable to resist the pull any longer, they finally surrender to everything, the force being too great to keep them simply ... friends. But how long can their happiness last?

Someone from the past surfaces and Eva is left with a choice, the outcome of which can affect both of their lives. Can the secret she keeps ruin their future together? While Colton is convinced Eva is the one for him, will his own fears be their undoing? Staying together becomes harder when tragedy hits and the strength of their love is put to the ultimate test. Can they withstand the outside influences that continually threaten to tear them apart? Can one of them sacrifice their own happiness so that the other can fulfill their dream?

This is a coming of age love story. (YA) Recommended for ages 15+ due to language and sexual situations.

45074332R10172

Made in the USA
Middletown, DE
14 May 2019